PRAISE FOR VIVIAN AREND

"Vivian Arend does a wonderful job of building the atmosphere and the other characters in this story so that readers will be sucked into the world and looking forward to the rest of the books in the series."
~ *Library Journal*

"Steamy and sweet complete with a whole host of colourful side characters and enough sub-plots to get your teeth into. A fab read!"
~ *Scorching Book Reviews*

"There's a real chemistry between the characters, laced with humor and snappy dialogue and no shortage of steamy sex scenes to keep things lively. The result is an entertaining, spicy romance."
~ *Publishers Weekly*

Silver Mine is an outstanding story. The author creates a world that invites readers for the ride of their lives."
~ *Coffee Time Romance Reviews*

Arend offers constant action and thrills, and her characters are so captivating and nuanced that readers will have a hard time guessing who the villains really are.
~ *RT Book Reviews*

Granite Lake Wolves

Wolf Signs

Wolf Flight

Wolf Games

Wolf Tracks

Wolf Line

Wolf Nip

Takhini Wolves

Black Gold

Silver Mine

Diamond Dust

Moon Shine

Takhini Shifters

Copper King

Laird Wolf

A Lady's Heart

Wild Prince

A full list of Vivian's print titles is available on her website

www.vivianarend.com

COPPER KING

TAKHINI SHIFTER: BOOK 1

VIVIAN AREND

Copper King
Copyright © 2014 by Arend Publishing Inc.
ISBN: 9781989507889
Edited by Anne Scott
Cover by Croco Designs
Proofed by Sharon Muha

We are wild as colts unbroke, but never mean.
Of our sins we've shoulders broad to bear the blame;
But we'll never stay in town and we'll never settle down,
And we'll never have an object or an aim.
No, there's that in us that time can never tame;
And life will always seem a careless game.

"The Rhyme of the Restless Ones"—Robert Service

1

———

Jim Halcyon was in lust.

Or maybe *obsessed* was a better term.

Whatever it was, he couldn't pull his gaze away. Her bright coppery tones reflected the overhead lights, sparkling back as she rotated before him. Soft edges, infinite value—not because she was so rare, but because of what she represented.

This time, she wasn't getting away from him.

"You're the easiest person in the world to distract," Damon Black taunted.

Jim instinctively closed his fingers over the coin lying in the palm of his hand, tempted to slam the fist he'd formed into the pretty-boy face of one of the only shifters brave enough to mock him.

His best friend peeled his grasp open and withdrew the small copper disk, placing it and its protective plastic case on the bar counter in front of them. "Now that you've seen for yourself Lady Luck is here, let's talk. How have you been? I haven't seen you much in the past month, and

I

phone calls and texts don't cut it, since you suck at doing anything other than yattering about work."

"I've been busy," Jim snapped.

Damon raised a brow, his unspoken *see what I mean?* coming through loud and clear.

Jim let out a long, slow breath. Fine, he'd humour the blond bastard. "You know, for someone who swears he wants me to relax, you might let a fellow have some quality time with the woman he loves, instead of rushing the moment." Jim deliberately lifted the coin in the air, twisting slowly so the casino lighting bounced off the cut lines, making the ancient artifact shine like a brand-new penny.

"Fine by me." A gloating grin drifted over Damon's fair features. "Since this is the only time you'll get a chance to fondle her, you may as well make the most of it."

"Ass."

Damon chuckled. "Three years running I've won the bet. You must miss having Lady Luck in your life."

Jim forced down a growl of discontent, but facts were facts. It wasn't because he hadn't done his damnedest to win, and no way Damon could claim otherwise.

The trouble was every man had a fatal flaw, and Jim Halcyon's was women. Blonde, brunette, short or tall, there was so much to love about women. Plus, there were so many women to love, and Jim happily obliged as many as possible.

His dedication to the task had inevitably led to his downfall during their previous contests. Not because he'd been fucking around, but because every damn time he'd ended up acting as a white knight to some damsel in distress. He had no proof, but he was almost certain the ladies had been setups put in place by his rival.

Damon might be a great friend, but the joker never gave an inch.

Not about anything—and lately his neurotic energy seemed focused on *make Jim relax*. It was like being friends with an overenthusiastic border collie.

Other years their challenges had taken them around the world to all sorts of exotic locations. They'd wined, and dined, and partied like animals as well as completing their task. This time, though, the lucky piece was the only part of the competition Jim was interested in, as he'd informed his friend months ago. Set up something fast and to the point— make it over quickly so Jim could get back to work a.s.a.p.

Damon had refused to give up any advance details, damn near dragging him to Vegas and holding Lady Luck as bait until Jim finally agreed to show up without specifics.

"This year's going to be different," Jim insisted. "I refuse to get caught up in any sob stories that might steal victory from me. Let's get rolling. What's the challenge?"

Damon gave him a long, hard stare, his bright blue eyes far too astute. "Dude, stop and breathe for a minute. You can't keep going like a madman or you're going break something. Or someone."

"Exactly. So hurry up and let's start relaxing."

Damon rolled his eyes.

"I'm winning her back," Jim warned.

His friend shook his head slowly, as if realizing something. He spoke in a far softer voice. "It is just a game, right? A chance for us to let off some steam. You don't really believe your luck for the coming year depends on winning the coin?"

"Of course not," Jim denied, shoving down memories that threatened to rise. "I don't believe in luck."

"Ha!" His friend's response, instant and loud, brought the attention of others their way. Mostly smiles, especially from the women as Damon turned the single outburst into a rolling laugh, the kind that was contagious. "Do you want me to get you a shovel to handle that load of shit?"

Oh, the joys of friends who have known you for years. "It's not really that I think I have shitty luck without her."

"Okay." Which also meant *bullshit*.

Jim briefly wondered what Damon would look like as a rug.

Vengeful thoughts temporarily on hold, Jim rolled the coin between his fingers like a street performer. A low hum of conversation and music surrounded them with the constant din unique to Vegas. Slot machines sang, bells and thrills echoed, accompanied by the occasional burst of laughter or raised voices. Piped-in oxygen wafted on the air. All of it as familiar as his own backyard.

Hell, this was his backyard—one of them, anyway. The luxury suite on the thirty-sixth floor had his name on the lease, same as the penthouse apartment he owned in New York, and the spectacular new home going up on his family inheritance in the north.

The memory jerked him to a stop—

There were things he didn't want to dwell on, and that was one of them.

So he forced a grin back on his face and went to work distracting Damon. "I just happen to have even more spectacular luck than usual when she's in my possession. I was the one who found her all those years ago."

"I know. I get to hear this story every damn year. An old woman foretold your future and called you the Copper King. Blah, blah, blah." Damon shook his head sadly, as if ready to call the men in white for a visit. "She's a figment of your imagination, Jim. You were drunk."

"Me? If I was drunk, how come you don't remember how we got back to the ship?" Eighteen years old, and they'd spent the summer running rampant through the Mediterranean. It was the best graduation present his parents could have given him.

Another hard slam to his gut. Another fake smile pinned to his lips.

Damon?

Laid a hand on his shoulder, as if the bastard knew exactly what was going through his brain.

Jim lifted his glass in a silent salute to his parents before shooting the liquid back, the cold burn settling in like a familiar fire. Seize the moment—it's what they would have wanted. It was part of the reason they'd given him such freedom so many years ago.

And the summer hadn't all been partying and fooling around…

Well, it had *mostly* been partying and fooling around, but there had been two other noteworthy accomplishments. The acquisition of the ancient coin he and Damon had pooled their rapidly dwindling resources to purchase, *and* Jim had gotten a good look at all the different architecture.

He'd come back inspired, not only from the Copper King prophecy bouncing in his head, but with the belief he could do anything he applied himself to.

Including becoming rich building others' dreams.

Richer. He might have been born into money, but he'd more than doubled his initial stake since putting his mind to the task.

At his side, Damon swirled his whiskey, his smile broadening. "That summer will live on in infamy." He glanced at Jim. "Whether the fortuneteller was right or not, we've had our moments, haven't we? I mean all things considered, who would have guessed that a wolf and a bear could go as far as we have in the last dozen years?"

Jim raised his second drink in the air. "It's only going to get better."

Damon clinked their glasses together, and they both drank, the icy liquor flowing down Jim's throat in a rush that turned to liquid flames.

Having a wolf shifter as a best friend wasn't typical, but then neither Jim nor Damon were typical shifters. Rather than hang out with the wolf pack, Damon tended more toward the loner side of the equation. And most bears, who were better known for enjoying seclusion, didn't understand why Jim enjoyed constantly having company around.

He liked time alone well enough, but crowds made him surprisingly happy. And women—

Because these days it always came back to the women. They were his distraction, and thus his salvation.

On the other side of the round bar, two nicely packaged ladies were eyeing them, lashes fluttering as they sipped their drinks and whispered together in low tones.

Damon noticed them noticing, a low approving rumble escaping as he motioned for the bartender. He ordered a pitcher of beer then turned back to Jim. "The blonde on the right thinks you're exceptionally sexy, by the way. She wants to slurp you up in one go."

Jim choked in mid-drink. "You should come with a warning sign. It's not fair wolf hearing is that much better than humans'."

"You're just complaining because you can't hear for shit."

"Fuck off."

His hearing was better than a typical human, just not as good as a wolf. Another delight of having old friends—the arguments carried on for years. "You want me to open a can of whoop-ass on you?"

His friend twisted in his chair. "Ignoring for a brief moment the all-too-desirable damsels who are flirting with us, are you ready for this year's challenge?"

"I take it we're not canoeing the length of the Yangtze River?" He'd come so close to winning last year, he'd been positive Damon wouldn't dare another physical challenge. Yet here they were in Nevada. "We're trekking across the desert, right? No food, no water. A true Survivorman in the best tradition of shifterdom."

"Unfortunately, there are a few too many satellites perusing this section of the state. I don't think we want anyone wondering why there's a grizzly trekking through the area. Hell, do you want to end up hit by another tranquilizer dart?"

Jim chuckled over a previous year's disaster. "I never expected the RCMP to find us that far north in Québec."

"You're lucky I figured out which zoo they took you to after you got caught." Damon put his empty glass on the bar. "No, since I am the previous winner and get to set the challenge, I've worked hard to make it perfect. I considered organizing a game of wits—"

"Admitting defeat already, are you? Since you're unarmed?"

Damon ignored his interruption. "—and instead decided that, come Friday, we'll be biking to Crater Lake and back."

Wait. "Okay, the biking thing works for me, as long as you're talking motorbikes, but what the hell? Why did you tell me to get here on Monday if this doesn't go down until Friday?"

"Can I borrow your phone for a second?"

Jim stifled his second *what the hell* and handed it over. "Not answering my question is immature. What gives?"

His friend shrugged, poking briefly at the phone. "I figured you need one thing right now. Time off."

"Right. I'll take the day off to do the ride."

"And you'll dive right back into work the next day."

"So?" Jim glared, daring him to keep pushing.

Like the moonstruck-crazy wolf that he was, Damon only grinned harder. "So, consider this an enforced vacation. From now until we hit the road, you're off the clock. You're in Vegas. Play some games, find someone to screw. Have some fun."

Damn it. His friend was asshole enough to force him to have a good time. "This is bullshit, Damon. Give me back my phone."

"Sure."

Jim watched in shocked disbelief as Damon deliberately dropped his lifeline to work into the beer pitcher the waiter had just set on the counter.

"You *shit*."

Damon hauled the container out of reach before Jim could rescue his technology. "I know you have nothing vital in the works, because you had no idea where I would take us. Which means, as completely obsessive as you are, you cleared your calendar for the week. Suck it up and have a good time for a change."

It was damn near impossible to stay angry with the loco wolf. "You owe me a new phone, and a new pitcher of beer."

"Deal." Damon thrust out a hand. "First thing when we get back from the road trip, I'll buy you one with all the bells and whistles."

Jim gave in and gave up, shaking his friend's hand. It

wasn't that bad an idea—spending a couple days hanging out with the bastard. "We haven't done this for a long time."

"Maybe you haven't, but I'm fully up to speed with all my moves, and ready for the next round." Damon eased back his chair, tilting his head toward the women, making it obvious what kind of action was on his mind.

Hell, yeah. Jim made eye contact with the ladies who sized him up as if he were a tasty piece of cake. One of them licked her lips, and a hit of sexual heat rolled through his gut. If Damon insisted he had to stay and play?

Playing could be fun.

He slapped a pile of bills on the counter, motioning for the bartender. "Tell the ladies their drinks are on me."

Jim planted a hand between Damon's shoulders and forcibly directed him around the corner of the elevated bar. The women watched, rosy-cheeked and obviously pleased at their approach.

"Who says you're out of practice?" Damon elbowed him in the ribs. "You're such a dog."

"Look who's talking, wolfboy."

His friend didn't argue. In fact, he slipped between the women easily, hands landing on their shoulders as he kicked into flirtation mode.

With devoted attention to his task, Damon didn't notice Jim jerk to a complete stop, captured by the most mesmerizing sight on the casino floor.

Sensual curves topped by absolute concentration, the woman's gaze was fixed on a poker table. Her face was unconventionally beautiful, with high cheekbones and a crooked mouth, the corners of which were curled into a smile that screamed mischief.

Jim unlocked his feet from where they'd frozen to the

ground, drifting forward slowly so he could get a closer look at his wonderful discovery.

Her hair was incredible. Long strands of spun reddish-gold, fresh from Rumpelstiltskin's wheel, the shimmering mass brushed past her shoulders. The tiny diamond in her earlobe flashed in the lights as she stroked a loose strand behind her ear.

He wanted to see if her locks were as crushably soft yet silkily strong as the strands of copper they reminded him of. The copper he had, in his early years of construction, painstakingly handled, coiling old wire into bundles to be resold.

He'd made part of his millions touching copper, and right now all he wanted was to touch copper again.

A pleasant anticipation shot through his limbs, and his bear rumbled awake.

She was short, petite even. The size of woman he could scoop up with one arm and not even notice her weight, especially if she wrapped her arms around his neck.

Of course, that would lead to her putting her legs around his hips, and suddenly the images flashing into his brain were far more intriguing than the idea of hanging with Damon, even with the lovely ladies at the bar.

His mysterious woman licked her lips, and his groin tightened further. He stared at the moisture left behind on the plump surface as driving lust hit. He needed to taste her. Her lips, the curve of her neck. The sweet swell of her breasts.

His cock pressed rock hard against the front of his dress pants, and he damn well planned to do something about that. Very soon.

A brief, blinding concern struck—everything about her wide-eyed innocence called to the protective side of him.

He didn't want to simply fuck her a few times. He wanted to wrap his arms around her, bending low to protect her from the sight of everyone else as he took the first taste of her rose-tinted pout. But *no way* would another woman come between him and winning this challenge.

Which led to a conversation between his lust and his ambition. Jim never understood why other people talked about having angels and devils on their shoulders to work out moral dilemmas.

All he had was one raunchy bastard and one filthy fucker, and it was scary how fast they got to the point.

It's only Monday. You have until Friday.

This is just about getting her into bed.

Of course. And in the shower. And up against the wall.

Go get her...

He took another top-to-bottom perusal, his amusement rising after spotting the neon-green shoes on her feet. Pale grey pants clung to her legs, rounding over the flair of her hips. Her top was white with what looked like teeny polka dots scattered on the material, a hoodie in the back. The cut of the front was modest, but he'd easily fix that by slipping a couple buttons loose to better appreciate her full breasts. For someone who would barely come up to his chin, she was built just how he liked.

Now all he had to do was convince her to time with him.

Damon insisted he relax? He knew exactly how, and with whom, he planned to relax with.

2

In the thirty minutes since she'd slipped into the casino, Lillie had been rubbernecking like crazy, unable to decide where to look first. She'd seen pictures of Vegas online, and watched the live-camera panoramas, but the reality was far more exciting than a flat-screen image, even a multi-screen HD setup like she'd done her research on.

It had taken some wrangling to get to this point, but now that she was finally here, she was going to enjoy herself to the fullest.

Hopefully without freaking out in the process.

Buzzzzz.

She pulled her phone from her pocket, peeking at the incoming text message. Addie. Bloodhound in training—she should have known her best friend wasn't about to let her off the hook that easy.

You still alive? Been captured by pirates?

Lillie laughed softly as she entered her response. *This isn't Disney, it's Vegas*

Disney has giant mice. You hate mice

Which is why Vegas now has another bear. For a few days, at least. I'm fine—nothing has changed since I texted you from the airport

Lillie tucked herself against the side of a slot machine, glancing around at the increasing number of people in the area. She was getting hungry, and perhaps it was time to take a break from the floor before her inner bear woke and got scared.

Text me if you need anything, hon. Anything. You're crazy, but you're my crazy

And that? Was what made Addie so special. Loyal and trustworthy to the end. *Awww, thanks. I promise to keep in touch*

With her stomach's growing need in mind, Lillie shoved her phone back in her pocket and lifted her chin, scenting the air for the best direction to head. She'd grab some supper...maybe even take in a show.

Finding someone to have a final fling with was also on her bucket list, but low. Really low. The concept sounded like fun, but she wasn't very good at flings, at least not in real life.

In her imagination? *That* was a different story. In her fantasy life, she was the queen of dirty interludes.

She glanced around the casino floor, taking in the flashing lights and loud noises as she mentally scrolled through some of the amazing romps she'd conjured up without a lick of trouble. Her perfect man flashed to mind. Dark and mysterious, sexy enough to set her heart pounding, but kind and understanding...

Actually in the fling-planning department, she'd focus on the *sexy and he knows what to do with it* instead of the bit about remembering birthdays and bringing her flowers.

She wanted someone to sweep her off her feet and rock her world all night long.

Like that was ever going to happen.

Her gaze stuttered to a stop at the approach of one of the finest masculine specimens she'd seen in her life, as if her fantasy man had come to life. Maybe this *was* like Disneyland, where all her dreams could come true.

When you wish upon a star...

Dream or not, watching the dark-haired man stalk down the casino aisle was an exercise in sheer pleasure.

He didn't simply walk, or stroll lazily from side to side like any of the other gamblers. It was as if each stride he took was deliberate. Not an inch to the left or right he didn't intend. And at every step, his tailored suit shifted casually on his broad shoulders, the crisp white shirt underneath open at the collar.

Hmm, that was extra nice. If he'd worn a tie, he would have looked more businesslike. Solemn and stately. Hunky as ever, in the sharply cut suit, but...

Something about the missing tie turned the yummy eye candy up to eleven. As if he'd unknotted the black silk, pulling it off slowly. Drawing it through his hand in a sensual tease before wrapping the *still warm from his body* fabric around his willing partner's wrists, then calmly tying her to the headboard of his bed.

Or maybe he'd begun undressing in anticipation of ravishing someone, which changed the rest of his outfit into a *dress code be damned* attitude.

The predator visible in every inch of his body was attempting to camouflage itself, hiding until the moment when the polished veneer would slide away, and he'd explode into a furious, hungry animal, possessiveness in his grasp...

Whoa, nelly.

Lillie blinked hard, hand pressed to her chest as she fought to slow her breathing. It had gotten a touch out of control as she'd slipped into her fantasy world. Damn, she needed to take up writing fanfic or something, she was making herself sweat.

Still, with the scruff on his chin, his aristocratic nose, his firm lips pressed together determinedly—she wasn't imagining the kind of deliciousness he would be in starring in one of her daydreams. Not to mention the intense gaze in his dark eyes as he stared at her as if she were his prey and—

That's when she finally clued in that all those deliberate steps were bringing Mr. Dark and Dangerous straight toward *her*.

The thump of her guilty heart was hard enough to rock her entire body. Phooey, had she been discovered already?

There was no reason to assume the little slip-away she'd pulled from her scheduled agenda would continue to be successful, but this was far too soon to give up the adventure. It had taken an incredible amount of luck to get to Vegas in the first place.

Only, as the drool-worthy dark-eyed man narrowed the distance between them, it grew clearer he wasn't some security guard who'd figured out she wasn't where she was supposed to be.

And the closer he got, the more she realized whether or not he was a security guard, coming face-to-face with that intense of a man was not on her current wish list.

Lillie twirled on the spot and made a rapid retreat, damn near jogging down the open center of the aisle before darting sideways between rows of penny slots. She took five paces forward and cut to the left, five more then to the right, moving as rapidly as possible, zigzagging her way through the casino.

Thank goodness she had on runners instead of high heels. It didn't matter that she must look totally undignified, as long as she didn't get caught.

Slipping between crowds of people, ducking around machines. Whatever it took to get her away from the man who had eyed her as if she were the only thing on his agenda for the next twenty-four hours.

The only thing on the menu.

She slammed to a stop, digging into her pocket for some change as she turned her back to the room. Maybe she could hide in plain sight.

Lillie slipped a coin into the machine and pushed the big square button on the right, not even caring what she was playing. Not worrying about anything but keeping under the radar.

The electronic tickers on the screen rolled past in imitation of the old-fashioned one-armed bandits. Odds of making any money were low—she'd have gone with blackjack if she'd wanted to win. Black-box technology definitely put the odds in the house's favour.

All most people would notice were the spinning colours, which she ignored, slipping another coin into the slot as she cautiously examined the machines on either side of her. Her nearest neighbours didn't even glance her way, they were so obsessed with their games.

Lillie caught a flash of her reflection, biting back a snarky comment at her stupidity. She jerked up the hoodie on her top. If anything was going to give her away, it would be her distinctive hair colour.

She continued to feed coins into the machine, the bells and whistles seeming to grow louder every time she pressed the button, but she was too busy trying to peer around without *looking* as if she was frantically peering around to see if anyone was about to pounce.

Her bear grumbled uneasily. According to that side of Lillie's psyche, this entire trip was just plain nasty.

Nap soon? her bear suggested. *Somewhere quiet?*

Why the human side had insisted on making a trip in February in the first place was beyond the animal's comprehension. As a shifter, she didn't have to do something silly like hibernate, but it took a whole lot more to convince her bear to come out during the winter.

Add in voluntarily tossing herself into a crowded room with all sorts of humans and shifters milling around? Her bear did the equivalent of wrapping its furry arms around itself, and hunkered down to pout.

Lillie didn't have time at the moment to deal with herself. Her heart still pounded, the grumbly action in her belly now caused more from nerves than from hunger.

But it appeared she might be out of the woods, stalker-wise.

Another push on the button.

Another coin.

She took a deep breath and let it out slowly, glancing over her shoulder for a last check. Could it be she was safe? She was ready to head to the safety and quiet of somewhere far, far away.

Without another peek at the game, she turned, gaze darting from side to side to ensure she was in the clear.

And then it happened. At her back, a siren began to wail.

She whirled in time to see flashing lights erupt from the top of her machine. She reached out, frantic to turn off whatever she had triggered. Desperate to stop the loud and obtrusive noises that were drawing attention from all over the casino, but there were no control keys to use—no computer override to access.

Simply the word *JACKPOT* flashing off and on in glowing neon colours.

Oh dear. This was terrible, this was horrible. Lillie backed away from the machine as if it were made of scorpions.

"Woohoo, good for you," the woman on her left said, rising from her stool and patting Lillie on the shoulder.

"Holy cow. One hundred thousand dollars?" The man on her right moved in as well, clapping his hands and cheering loudly.

They weren't the only two. It seemed everyone in the area was abandoning their machines and coming forward, closing in around her. Blocking off all of her escape routes and sucking the oxygen from the air.

She couldn't breathe. Her bear rumbled upward, clawing at her to demand they run. Every move Lillie made bumped her into someone, helpful hands pushing her back toward the impossibly loud and frightening machine.

Maybe if she closed her eyes that would make things better. Stars hovered against the blackness of the insides of her eyelids as she tried desperately to keep a full-blown panic attack from overwhelming her.

She was no longer worried about being discovered in the wrong place. Now all she wanted was to put space between her and the people crowding far too close.

Her bear pushed to the surface as she cried in fear, and Lillie covered her face with her hands, fighting the urge to shift right then and there. That was the last thing she needed, but it was close to becoming her only choice.

Lillie trembled on the edge of disaster when a

commanding voice broke through the chaos, ordering the crowds away. She found herself wrapped in strong arms, a hand holding her face to a solid wall of muscle.

"Everyone back to what you were doing. She's fine."

"She's better than fine," someone called. "She won the jackpot."

"So she did." Her mysterious savior's voice rumbled up from his chest, soothing over her like a warm blanket. Lillie snuck her arms around her rescuer and clung tightly. The heat from his chest—that solid wall she'd hidden against—soothed her human panic.

Her bear, however, was agitated beyond belief. Lillie struggled to keep her other side from taking over, but the beast wasn't ready to give up the fight.

Another low rumble struck her like a command, and her bear froze. Strong fingers continued to cradle the back of her head, holding her motionless. "Relax, sweetheart. I'll take care of things."

She took a deep breath, and exactly *what* he was hit her. The scent that filled her head was oh-so-masculine, while the strength of his shifter side registered loud and clear. Her bear wiggled its ears for a moment, considering this new thing.

Well, not its *literal* ears, because that would have been very uncomfortable.

She had to answer him. Warn him she wasn't safe yet. Even curled against him, her fingers tangled in his shirt, she was on the verge of breaking apart. If he'd wanted to abandon her at that point, he would've had to peel her from his body.

It took all her strength to form the word. "Scared."

"I noticed."

She could have sworn he pressed his lips to the top of

her head, but she had her eyes squeezed shut, so she couldn't be certain.

He gave a few more orders, snapping out the words, clear and precise. Lillie felt the fool for not standing up for herself, but there was a line, and she'd gone too close to it. Letting him deal with the others meant she'd be less likely to cause a terrible incident.

When he lifted her in the air like some old-timey maiden being rescued from a swoon, she didn't protest. With how lightheaded she felt, it wasn't far from the truth.

All she knew for certain was that as the voices faded, the bells and whistles slowly disappearing into the background, the urge to throw up also faded, and that was a good thing.

He had one strong arm curved around her, another under her legs. Lillie stretched up to clasp his neck, her other hand still buried under his jacket as she fisted the material at his back.

He smelt good. Like the tang of wood smoke mixed with the sharp cut of wintry air. Familiar and invigorating. Sensual and intoxicating. They were still moving forward rapidly. Her bear was no longer about to burst through her skin, but neither human nor beast were ready to relax.

Lillie cautiously opened her eyes, staring first at her rescuer's chest. At the white shirt that was now crumpled from her clutching fingers. His dark jacket hung open, one of her arms tucked under it, her other hand touching the crisp hairs at the back of his neck.

Her heart skipped a beat as her gaze took in the face of the same man she'd dashed away from earlier. She summoned her meager reserves of courage. "Where are you taking me?"

"Somewhere you can unwind."

Hmm. If he kept talking, that would help a whole lot. His voice rumbled over her, vibrating deep in her ears and sending ricocheting pulses back and forth over sensitive nerve endings.

He pushed through a door, continuing to move forward at a good clip. Lillie squirmed upright to risk a peek at where they were. One deep breath was all it took to let her know they were now surrounded by shifters.

Which made this room a better place to be, but not much.

Her gaze paused for a moment on a cougar who lay sprawled over a couch, bacon-wrapped scallops being dropped into his mouth one after another by his patient partner in human form.

To their right, outside a long glass wall, was a fenced-in swimming pool, a section of parachute-cloth roof strategically arranged to allow the sunshine in while providing privacy from curious watchers above. Instead of beach chairs, soft cushions littered the edge, and assorted minks, ferrets and bobcats were curled up in the sun. A couple, one in human form, the other paddling big panther paws into the stream, floated on inner tubes around the lazy river.

Paradise arranged for the shifter set.

She took it all in at a moment's glance, but there were still too many people, and Lillie shuddered, pressing her face against her dark stranger once again.

Jim lowered himself into a chair as he cradled her close. He hadn't expected this when he'd gone to say hello to his beautiful distraction.

In fact, tracking her down had been fun. His bear didn't mind a little hide and go seek. But he'd spotted her a moment before she triggered the jackpot. Anxiously looking around as if someone were about to toss a net over her head. And the sheer desperation that had followed—

No, he'd been in exactly the right place at the right time. She'd been on the verge of shifting in public, and that was trouble in itself. He would have helped any fellow shifter in dire straits, but saving his mysterious beauty...

So much for not getting involved.

I have until Friday.

Don't forget that, his ambition urged.

As if he could forget. He knew what his trouble was. He had a hero complex, that's what. And since he did, he might as well go on and enjoy it.

He looked down at her, quite happy she'd continued to cling to him. "You feeling better?"

She nodded once before shaking her head vigorously. "Too many people. Too much power."

Huh. He adjusted her to sit more comfortably, keeping hold of her head so she could only look at him and not into the room. "They're just shifters. I'm the scariest thing in here."

She had both hands on his shirtfront, palms pressed to his chest. He liked her caressing him, even if it was through a layer of fabric.

"I know," she whispered, "but my bear doesn't enjoy crowds."

He couldn't stop from laughing, softly so as not to spook her further. "Vegas might not be the best holiday destination for you, sweetheart."

Her shoulders lifted slightly. "It was my only chance, and I thought I could handle it."

The urge to touch was too tempting to resist any longer. Jim caressed his hand over her cheek, continuing back until his fingers made contact with her hair, fondling the shiny mass again and again as he smoothed out the rough spots. Petting her with long, slow strokes until she let out a low breath, body relaxing.

"There we go. You're safe."

A contented sigh escaped her. The sound was a bugle call, waking up his cock all over. Jim liked the feel of this sweet honey in his arms, all soft and warm. He was ready to take her somewhere, strip her and return to this position. Maybe with her knees on either side of his hips, so he'd be able to cup her ass and help her ride.

His bear rumbled in interest. His human agreed—his cock was harder now than before, but he had to do the right thing and make sure she wasn't with a partner already.

"Is there someone I should call?"

Instant response. She jolted upright as if she'd been plugged into an electric source. "Oh no. That's fine. I'm good now. Thank you for all your help."

When she would have crawled off him, Jim resisted, holding her with firm care. "Let me take you to your room, then. You need to give your bear a time-out so you don't do something foolish."

Her eyes widened before she pulled herself under control. Her gaze twisted toward the ceiling as she closed her mouth and chewed her lower lip frantically.

Obviously his package of trouble was trying to come up with a convincing lie. This was getting more entertaining by the minute.

"I'll be fine," she repeated. "Thank you for rescuing me though." She glanced down, her hands slowly retreating from his chest as she attempted to wiggle away.

"At least let me come with you to get your winnings. You need a guard if you're going to collect that amount of money."

He watched her mouth move, positive a silent *oh shit* escaped her pouting lips. "That's right. The money."

"Yes, the money." More entertaining by the minute, indeed. "Did you not intend on winning money in Vegas?"

"Not that much." She slapped a hand over her mouth.

Now Jim was completely intrigued. No way would he allow this woman out of his sight, not only because everything about her called to him, but she was so damn amusing. "Well, it looks as if it's your lucky day. What's your name, sweetheart?"

"Lillie."

"And mine is Jim. You okay to go for a walk?"

This time when she tried to rise, he let her go, waiting patiently and admiring every move she made as she straightened her clothing and patted her hair behind her ears. Standing between his legs, her hazel-green eyes were nearly in line with his as she wiggled and tugged, adjusting the soft fabric of her hoodie back over that ample chest.

For the first time he noticed what the polka dots actually were. Her top had teeny teddy bears all over it, and he smiled.

Smiled even harder when she finished tidying herself and turned her attention on him. Smoothing the wrinkles from his shirt with her hands, shaking her head in dismay as she adjusted his collar and tugged his suit jacket back into position. "I'm sorry. I seem to have gotten you ruffled up."

"You go right ahead and ruffle me anytime you want."

Her gaze shot to meet his, eyes widening and cheeks brightening with a rosy flush. "Oh..."

Damn if she wasn't the most charming thing he'd seen

in a long time. "In fact, if you're interested in a little more *ruffling,* I have no problem with helping."

A hesitant swallow. Eyes turned downward. "I think I'd like that."

Soft, but clear.

Jim took her by the hand and led her from the room, intrigued to discover where this lovely diversion would take him. It wasn't what he had expected to be doing right now, but hell if he wanted to stop.

3

———

*W*hy?

Why did she have to be so damn lucky?

It was a good thing Jim had been there to help save the day, but it wouldn't have been necessary in the first place if she could have won some measly amount, like twenty bucks, or fifty. But *no...*

She glanced over her shoulder at the room they had just left. "Do all the casinos have shifter-friendly sections? I did as much research as possible, but only heard about invitation-only rooms."

"It's simpler to get in when you know somebody, but, yes, pretty much every hotel has a safe spot, whether the owners know it or not." He gestured around them. "The Luxor has the most shifter-friendly setup. It's owned by the head of the Northern American tigers, and she's made sure to provide lots of comforts for the creatures who come to play. But I like the Bellagio the best."

He led them through the maze of the casino floor, keeping to scantily occupied areas, a kindness for which Lillie was grateful. It took less time than she'd imagined to gather her winnings and tuck the cheque safely into her wallet. "Thank you for helping me."

He squeezed her fingers, catching her gaze and winking as they left the cashier box and headed farther into the hotel. "You'll find I'm a very helpful fellow. I'm good at all sorts of things."

Her imagination went off, and this time there didn't seem to be any reining it in. "You're not here with anyone, are you?"

Jim shook his head. "Well, not with any ladies, if that's what you're asking. My friend Damon is somewhere around, but you don't need to meet him."

The growly tone he used on the last statement sent a shiver up her spine. "What's wrong with him?" she whispered.

The big bear slowed, pulling her toward him and tucking her against an empty section of wall. He caught her fingers in his hand, lifting her knuckles to his mouth. His lips pressed briefly to her skin, and a lovely shot of adrenaline raced along her arm until it zapped her in the heart.

If her heart had been located directly between her legs.

"Damon is a scalawag. Terrible heartbreaker. I, on the other hand, am the perfect gentleman.

She knew a line when being fed it. A smile twisted her lips. "Of course you are. I could sense that."

"Before or after you decided to run away from me?"

Interesting position she'd gotten herself into. Her back to the wall, her tall stranger leaning an arm on either side of her body as he locked her in place. A slight edge of fear still trembled, but he'd proved himself trustworthy enough that she smoothed her hands up his shirt, not bothering to answer his question with words.

"You're not planning to run away anymore."

The human side of her didn't plan on it, but her shy other self could be an issue. "You're a grizzly," she whispered.

He stared for a long moment, his dark brown eyes flashing with amusement. "You have a problem with my bear?

Lillie shook her head. "Not me, but he might have to do some sweet-talking to convince my bear not to freak out."

"You have no problem with me, though." He played with her hair, twisting a lock around his finger.

"Nope. I already said I don't mind some mussing up." Where had that bold statement come from? It was true, but still...

His cocky smile widened. "I think I'll call you Trouble."

"What? You're not going to call me red or carrots or something equally annoying?"

"Because of your hair? Hell, no, the colour is gorgeous." He wouldn't stop playing with it, his gaze fixed on his fingers as he tugged again. "I want something special to call you when I wrap this in my fists and make you scream in pleasure."

Well now.

She wanted to lift a hand and fan her face after that, but instead she caught the front lapels of his jacket and held on tight. "Is the screaming planned for anytime soon? Because I totally say yes, but I need some supper first. I would hate to pass out for the wrong reason."

He stroked her cheek. "Damn, I love being a bear."

She giggled, her amusement impossible to contain. "For any particular reason? I mean, I like my bear too, when she isn't making my life crazy by going loco on people, or wanting to take naps at inconvenient times."

"I love that I can come right out and tell you I want you."

True. "Shifters do get to enjoy good, clean fun."

"Or not so clean, if you do it right."

She slid her hands up the soft fabric of his suit jacket, loving the slick of it against her skin. She stretched all the way until her fingers were wrapped around his neck, then tugged.

Jim came obediently toward her.

Or maybe she was mistaken, because he stopped an inch shy of their lips meeting, and that was not her intention.

Not. At. All.

"I love being a bear," he repeated. "Because it means I can see you, know I want to drive you wild all through the night, and I don't have to play games to get there. But the other thing I love?"

He moved in closer. Closer. A rush of warm air brushed her cheek as he skipped her lips and directed his words toward her ear.

"I love being a bear because I'm a bossy bastard, and being a grizzly pretty much means I get my way."

A delicious shiver raced up her spine at his dark, growly tone of voice.

"So, if that's not what turns you on, you should be a good girl. I'll take you back to your room, and later you can venture out to find a bunny rabbit to play with. Otherwise, I promise to take care of you, but I call the shots."

The temptation to lick his neck was so strong her fingers curled involuntarily, fisting in his hair, the soft texture crushed against her palms. "In bed? Or all the time?"

He didn't answer, not with words. Instead, that low rumble escaped his chest, the vibrations passing to where her breasts were pressed tight to him. Her nipples were the first to go, like an early-warning system, this one of lust, the nubs springing to full attention.

As the reverberation continued, warning bells went off in her belly, but it was too late. Her clit had already run up the white flag of surrender, all of her absolutely and completely ready for him to be a bossy bastard.

In bed and out, if that's what it took. Fantasy world, meet reality. For one brief moment in time, she intended to live her dream.

"Treat me nice, and you can be as bossy as you want."

He stood there silently, and she thought he might kiss her. Anticipation rose, her pulse pounding so hard stars floated before her eyes.

Instead, he brushed his cheek against hers as he pulled away, the scruff on his jaw leaving a lovely ticklish sensation that kick-started the butterflies in her stomach all over.

Jim held out his hand. "What type of food do you like?"

"Surprise me."

He should have known his evening wouldn't keep rolling as smoothly as he'd hoped. He wasn't that lucky, not with Damon around. Jim had barely gotten Lillie settled in a quiet, intimate seating area, drinks on the way as he wrapped his arm around her and pulled her close.

"Tell me what you're doing in Vegas. It sounds as if this is your last hurrah or something."

She opened her mouth, that hint of hesitation showing, but before any lies could come out—

"This is where you got to." Damon dropped himself onto the bench on the other side of Lillie.

"Go away," Jim ordered.

His friend only grinned harder, smiling at Lillie as if he'd just discovered the female race. "Well, aren't you the most delightful thing. And look, you're here, sitting with one of the most boring individuals on the face of the planet. I'm so glad I came to save you."

Lillie fluttered a few times. "Hi. You must be Damon."

Jim laughed.

At least he did until instead of looking shocked, Damon sat back and nodded approvingly. "I can see Jim has already been singing my praises. My reputation precedes me."

"If you don't get out of here, your head will be preceding your body out the front door." Jim adjusted the silverware on the table, curling tighter around Lillie.

Damon arched one brow in the Vulcan imitation he saved for special occasions. "Someone's getting all possessive and growly and stuff. Now I'm even happier I found you two."

"Choose now," Jim warned. "You can stay, or you can keep your teeth."

Under his arm Lillie's body shook slightly, and he quickly moved to check she was okay.

She was more than okay, her smile the brightest he'd seen since meeting her. "Are you hungry, Damon? Because we're getting a bite to eat."

Shit. "Damon is not hungry."

"Actually, I'm starving." Damon jerked the menu out of Jim's hands and peered at it intently. "I hear the steaks here are good."

Jim was ready to slice up his best friend and pop him on the barbecue when Lillie laid a hand on his thigh and snuggled closer. "You can share my menu," she offered.

She smiled up at him, and damn if there was any way

he could refuse those beautiful green eyes anything. "Fine. We can let the freeloader hang around during dinner."

"I'm paying," Lillie insisted.

Damon's amusement could be heard instantly. "You really think you can wrestle the bill from both of us?"

She was worrying her bottom lip. Jim placed a finger over it and stilled her. Leaning in, he brushed his lips over hers. On this issue, he agreed one hundred percent with Damon.

"Humour the big, bad predators," he murmured against her mouth, stealing another almost kiss as an appetizer. "We can afford it."

"So can I." She waved the banker's note in the air.

"Put it away."

"I'm not freeloading—"

"Stop protesting." Her attitude was damn refreshing, and he couldn't resist telling her so. "But I'm glad I don't have to worry that you're with me for my money."

Utter shock crossed her face at the suggestion. "Of course I'm not with you for your money."

Damon dropped his menu on the table and motioned for the waiter. "So, what are you with him for? Because I'm far better looking, and I'm not a bed hog."

Jim reconsidered his earlier leniency. His friend would look lovely on a spit. "Where would you like me to send your remains?"

Lillie laughed, tucking her fingers around Jim's biceps as she answered Damon. "I'll just have to take your word for that."

For how shy she had seemed earlier, Lillie loosened up during the meal, conversation flowing easily as Damon teased but backed off actually trying to seduce the woman.

They talked about the different menu choices. They

talked about the different games available in Vegas and laughed as Lillie rattled off the odds for each one. Hell, they even talked about the weather in a way that was entertaining.

The entire time they ate, though, Jim found it difficult to think about anything but what came next. It wasn't that it had been a long time since he'd been with a woman, but everything about Lillie enticed him.

And tormented him.

She lifted a piece of steak to her mouth, darting her tongue out to taste the surface before she placed the portion in her mouth. Jim's cock pressed against his zipper, and he adjusted position to gain some more room.

She picked up her bun and broke off a piece, slathering it with butter before popping the entire morsel into her mouth. The noises that followed made it sound as if she were one step away from climaxing right there in the restaurant.

Jim tore his eyes away from her lips, catching sight of Damon across from them. The wolf's jaw hung slightly open, his face flushed as he damn near panted.

Under the table, Jim kicked him. Hard.

Damon jerked out of range. "Oh, don't tell me you wouldn't be thinking the same thing if you were in my boots."

"Your boots had better start walking." Jim tilted his head toward the exit. They'd had enough sharing time, and his plans for the rest of the evening were not group activities.

Lillie glanced between them, the cutest expression growing as she puzzled over their discussion. "You don't want any dessert?"

A flash of mischief crossed his best friend's face. "You have no idea how much I'd love some dessert, but I'm being put on a diet. You kids have fun." Damon gave Jim a two-finger salute. "Let's meet tomorrow. I've got something for you."

"Deal." Anything to get the bastard away from the table as fast as possible. He waited until Damon's back disappeared out the wide open doors before calling for the bill.

"And you don't want dessert either. That is unexpected. Huh." Lillie was licking her fingers clean, and the aching need in Jim's gut shot from *want now* to *ready to explode*.

One after the other, the slim digits slipped between her lips. She swirled her tongue around them. Closed her mouth and pulled out with a *pop*.

He had her out of the restaurant and into an elevator before she had a chance to grab any dinner mints. The elevator doors closed, and he used his access key, desperately resisting temptation. He was not about to pick her up and push her to a wall, pinning her in place with his body as he ravished her lips.

Lillie stared at the corner of the small room. "They've got cameras in here, don't they?"

"Yup."

"Huh." She twirled to face him, cuddling under his jacket and nuzzling affectionately. "Thank you for dinner. And your friend Damon is funny."

"I'll make sure I tell him. Often. Because that's exactly what his ego needs. To be reminded that a beautiful woman thought he was funny."

She tilted her head back far enough he could peer into one hazel-green eye, the rest of her face still pressed to his chest as if she were cocooning. "Really?"

"Well, I sure as hell am not going to tell him you think he's sexy. Funny—that I can do. That's one step away from being called a good friend or a nice guy, both of which sting like death from a woman's lips."

The elevator doors opened on to his suite, and Jim gestured her forward. There were so many things he needed to consider. Which room should he take her in first? And on the bed? Floor? Couch?

But first he had to make sure his shy little bear got comfortable. He'd have to keep petting her until things were *juuuust* right.

4

———

*L*illie paced into the living room, admiring the beautifully decorated apartment.

Jim stopped by a low cupboard. "Take a look around," he ordered. "I'll grab us drinks."

Her heart was thumping as if she were a virgin about to be sacrificed on some sexual altar. She made her way to the windows, trailing her fingers over the back of the grey leather couch, its surface soft and cool to her touch.

Outside, the city spread in a circle, the glittering line of the Strip lit up and stretching into the distance. Taxis and cars with their white headlights and red taillights made interesting patterns as they moved in a synchronized manner.

Below them, the manmade lake was highlighted from all sides by brilliant spotlights. Jim's suite was in the exact location so when a spray of water shot skyward, it was perfectly visible. She pressed closer to the glass, watching eagerly.

"I saw this online," Lillie murmured. "The fountain shows. Too bad we can't hear the music."

"Who says we can't?" Jim's lips touched the side of her neck. He threaded his fingers through hers and brought her with him onto the balcony. Plants of all sorts covered the low concrete terraces on the exterior wall of the suite. Trickling waterfalls fell between the greenery, all of it a lush paradise in the middle of the desert.

Jim pressed a small button. The opening strains of "Con Te Partiro" rose from the speakers mounted above them. Lillie settled onto the cushiony loveseat Jim guided her to, her eyes glued to the show flawlessly displayed below.

"You can turn on the television to hear the music as well," Jim explained, "but since I prefer watching the real show outside, I had my own system installed. There's a radio transmitter tucked into one of the main speakers on the ground level that relays up to my suite."

He was pirating the signal. Lillie dragged her gaze from the show to examine him closer. "That sounds technical."

Jim shrugged. "The guy I hired said it was pretty easy."

Ahh. So Jim himself was not the hacker. His guy was right, if you knew what you were doing, it would be simple.

Lillie turned back to the performance, keeping her comment to herself.

The temperature was falling, but before it grew cool enough to feel a chill, Jim wrapped her in his arms, her body tight to his side as they reclined on the overstuffed cushions and enjoyed the show.

Her bear had more than woken up. With all the kerfuffle, the poor creature was no longer in its typical sleepy February frame of mind. As they sat quietly, that side of her tested the waters, wondering if Jim's grizzly planned to do something horrifying like eat her.

Lillie held her tongue. As a human, she was shy—she got that. But her bear took being a delicate beastie to an extreme. Still, they were intimately connected, and there was no arguing with this one.

Jim had to convince both sides of Lillie he was a safe bet.

He was doing a marvelous job so far. He had laid his arm along the back of the loveseat, her shoulders resting against his biceps. He draped his hand over her arm and held her lightly, tracing circles with his thumb. A gentle sweep back and forth as if he wasn't even aware he was doing it.

Her mouth had gone dry, and a whole lot of other places had gone wet, just from that touch.

She curled her legs up, her left knee rising slightly over his right leg. It was natural to lean her head on his chest as the music continued to serenade them. His chin brushed the top of her head, and he rubbed back and forth, matching the mesmerizing touch on her arm.

It was like a game of Operation, only he had no intention of avoiding hitting her buzzers. Every contact sent an electric pulse racing, shooting all directions until they careened together in a massive pileup directly over her clit.

Her bear was no longer afraid. Instead, the creature was sniffing around, curious why they were not pouncing upon this fascinatingly hunkalicious fellow.

Buzzz.

She jerked upright in surprise, far too slow in figuring out what was going on. She tugged her phone free and examined the text.

This is your breathing check. Please respond if you are able

A snort escaped as she turned to Jim. "Sorry, have to get this."

He gestured her to go ahead.

Addie's concern was cute, but her timing sucked. *What if I didn't answer?*

I'd be there so fast your pointy little head would spin

What if I was BUSY?

Addie added three dots in a row before coming back with *and are you likely to be "BUSY" anytime soon?*

Lillie went for broke. *Yes. I'm having a fling*

Oh sweetie

Not good. Not good when her best friend started with "Oh sweetie…"

You're too tenderhearted to go and fool around willy-nilly. This is a disaster waiting to happen

She screwed up her courage. *It's my last chance. I have to. I want to*

K. But call if you need me

She put away her phone, not as worried as she usually would have been after Addie had offered a warning.

Beside her, Jim adjusted his position, the heat in his eyes perfect for melting her final doubts.

"Are you ready to go in?" he asked.

He stood, bringing her to her feet. One hand slid around her back, guiding her into his apartment and the sea of pale blue walls and Mediterranean accents.

"It's so beautiful here."

"I like it." Jim pulled her away from examining a conch shell she'd found on the dining room table. "Lillie. I'm going to kiss you now."

The fact he'd thought to warn her only made it that much more unbearable to wait. They stood in the middle of the room, his hands rising to cup her face. Slowly he leaned in, tilting her head so when he touched their mouths together they were perfectly lined up.

For the first moment, his touch stayed soft and sweet, as

if he was cautious of not frightening her other side. She returned his kiss, licking into his mouth with her tongue for a second of torturous delight.

He waited, letting her explore before he took over, nibbling and tasting as if she were precious and fragile. Things rapidly heated up, and he kissed her far more hungrily. His mouth slid over hers in a sensual attack she had no way of escaping, and no desire to either.

When he nipped her bottom lip, she gasped, sighing with satisfaction as he eased the sting with his tongue. They were close enough she felt every inch of his muscular body.

He slipped one hand into her hair, the other down to rest on the upper curve of her butt, controlling her and holding her in place. It was impossible to keep from moving in response, undulating slowly, his cock hard against her.

Jim took his time kissing her, and it was lovely, and not nearly enough.

Then his target changed. His lips still nibbled and possessed, drifting along her jawline to her earlobe. He drove her wild, sending tingling sensations over her skin. His fingers dropped to the buttons of her shirt where he made short work of the tiny disks considering how big his hands were.

She clutched his biceps, the fabric of his suit smooth under her hands, but not what she wanted to caress. Even as he opened her blouse, Lillie flipped open his suit button and reached high to shove his jacket from his shoulders.

Jim raised an eyebrow. "I seem to have lost an article of clothing. Let's level the playing field."

His gaze dropped to the skin revealed by her open shirtfront. She shrugged out of the soft material, catching the shirt before it fell to the floor, instead tossing it on top of his coat.

She shivered under the intensity of his gaze as he took in her bare skin from waist to hairline, only the small bits covered by her lace bra still secret from him.

"Leave that on," he commanded.

Orders now? Oh yes, please. This was going to be a delightful evening. And Lillie suddenly knew exactly how she wanted to begin.

She'd gone over the list of fantasies she'd mentally orchestrated over the years, scrolling through the lot of them and looking for her absolute favourites.

The trouble was most of those had involved mysterious men with blank faces. They'd been extraordinarily wonderful in terms of saying the right things, and doing the right things, but they hadn't been real.

Faced with a very real, very solid grizzly bear who was staring at her as if she was delicious, none of the fantasies stood up to what she wanted to happen.

Which was fine, because she had said he could be in charge. Another lovely shiver tickled her from top to bottom. Exploring sex was always fun.

But until he did take over, she was going to play.

She caught hold of his belt in both hands. Pulled back on the leather and slipped loose the metal buckle. The long length came free with a sound like a soft exhale, or maybe that had been her. Carefully, she undid his button and lowered his zipper over the straining bulge.

Once again she couldn't decide where to look. Tilting her head back meant enjoying all the emotions flickering across his face. Desire, heat, mounting frustration as she moved infinitely slowly to pull his cock free.

That? Was the other fascinating direction to stare. As she released his pants, his erection greeted her. Commando. Lillie swallowed hard, stroking her palms over his length.

Soft skin and rising heat rubbed her fingers, a slight bit of moisture at the tip she captured with her thumb.

"You should see how big your eyes are. Like you just got the best present in the entire world." Jim's fingers were tangled in her hair, holding her so gently. "You don't have to do this."

"I'm pretty sure I do." Lillie slipped up on her tippy toes and pressed a kiss to his rough jawline. "Last hurrah, and all that. I definitely have this on my to-do list."

There were so many things she wanted, but with the thick length in her hands, his hips rolling slowly against her in a smooth rhythm, she could put the rest of them aside.

She dropped to her knees, the carpet warm under her.

It wasn't good enough for him. "If I were a better man I would stop you completely, but since I'm nowhere near that good..."

He scooped her up. Lillie squealed, laughing as he carried her. His open pants slipped down his hips as he brought her to the couch. They collapsed in a tangle of limbs until he settled her on the floor between his legs, a soft cushion under her knees.

His cock rose from a thatch of dark hair. Straining upward as he eased his shoulders back against the leather sofa. "Now you can go ahead. Have a blast."

He was joking, but she was honestly looking forward to having fun. She stroked him with both hands, increasing her pressure until he groaned, his eyes fixed on her, hands gripping the leather as if he were afraid to allow himself loose.

"I want to taste you," Lillie whispered.

"Dessert now being served."

Lillie leaned against the couch as she held his cock

vertical. She licked up one side, swirled her tongue around the head twice, then stroked down the other.

Jim hummed happily.

She did it again, only this time when she swirled her tongue she paused, wrapping her lips around the sensitive tip and pulsing.

Jim hummed, harder.

Teasing was fun, but it was time to move on. Lillie put her mouth over him and pushed down, getting him wet enough she could pump her hand over the root and suck on the sensitive head.

Jim's hum lost its stability, changing to a ragged *putt-putt-putt* noise.

A salty taste swirled through her mouth, and she swallowed, increasing suction as she pulled back. Increasing the pressure with her hand. He'd grown thicker in her fingers, stretching her mouth wider as she tried her best to please him.

She glanced up. Her mouth was full, hand moving rapidly, and his eyes had rolled back in his head. His hum turned into an all-out moan as he caught hold of her head, his hips shaking. The salty taste of come filled her mouth as he lost control.

Lillie sucked and pumped and played until Jim stopped her. Locking her in position as his climax faded.

She pulled off his cock with a satisfied smile. "I like the desserts they serve around here."

It was as if a whirlwind hit. One moment she was on her knees, the next she was sitting on the couch, her pants, undies and socks torn from her.

Cocky arrogance of the best sort on his face. "Pretty bit of trouble, aren't you?"

"Am I trouble?" She reached her arms over her head to grab the top of the backrest, the position pulling her breasts higher, still covered in see-through white lace.

He stared as if she were a priceless painting. "No trouble at all."

He leaned over and pressed a kiss to where her pulse was beating a tango in her throat.

The next kiss landed on her collarbone. The one after that along the edge where her bra and skin met, the upper slope of her breast tickled by the scruff on his chin.

When he pressed his lips to her nipple, she about shot off the couch. He opened his mouth and sucked both the fabric and the sensitive tip in. Using his tongue, he alternated licking with sucking until she grabbed his head, desperate to tear him away and remove the layer between them.

Trying to move him was like trying to move a brick wall.

His low laughter turned to a steady stream of cool air as he blew on the moistened tip, causing it to tighten further. "You wouldn't be trying to take control, would you? Because you've used up all your get-out-of-jail-free cards."

Somehow she found the courage to speak bluntly. "I want your mouth on my skin."

He smiled. "You said that so prettily, how can I refuse?"

Jim eased back far enough from his position between her legs to open room between them. He caught hold of her bra cup, folding the material in half to expose her nipple and the upper slope. He repeated the move on the other side, leaving her displayed and lifted to his eager mouth.

Lillie closed her eyes and let him play. Every touch added to the pressure building between her legs, pleasure wrapping itself around her with a familiar ache.

When he left her breasts to press a kiss to a spot beside her belly button, Lillie brought her hands from above her head, biting her fingers to stifle her scream of frustration. She didn't want him to stop what he was doing, but she need something more, and soon.

He adjusted his position, sliding his hands from her hips to her knees. "How flexible are you, sweetheart?"

Lillie stuttered for a moment. "Pretty good... Not sure. *Oh...*"

He'd pressed her knees farther apart before lifting them in the air so her hips were balanced on the edge of the couch, pussy totally exposed.

"Put your hands on your knees and hold your legs back."

There was no arguing with that tone of voice, and Lillie decided she'd have to be slightly mad to *want* to argue in the first place. She clutched her knees and held very still as he dragged his thumbs along her thighs until he touched her intimately.

Back and forth, a small motion, again and again Jim teased his thumbs through her folds, bringing moisture from her body on every other pass to tease her sensitive clit.

By the time he put his mouth on her, she was ready to break. The first contact of his tongue to her clit made her gasp. The second was like pulling a trigger, and her hips shot upward, tension shattering like ice on a sunny winter day.

Only he didn't stop. It was as if having made her come so quickly was a challenge, because he didn't stop. His tongue, his teeth. He glanced up, smiling with satisfaction, his grin wet from pleasing her.

Jim extended his hand to her lips. "Open your mouth."

She obeyed instantly, and he pressed two fingers over her lower lip and along her tongue, stroking back and forth twice before easing them apart so wetness coated every inch.

He growled as he watched her, and she closed her lips tighter, sucking and playing with her tongue against the thick digits. As he pulled them out, the heat in his dark brown eyes flashed.

Then he took his wet fingers and pushed them into her core. One, two, slipping in easily. A moan of pleasure escaped her and made him smile, their eyes locked together.

He pumped slowly at first then with increasing speed, curling his fingers against the front of her body. "You're going to come again before I take you. At least one more time."

Oh boy.

"We might be here for a while." She liked sex and all, but one orgasm a night was sufficient.

He twisted his fingers and lowered his talented tongue to the task, and suddenly she wasn't so sure about the one-orgasm-per-night limit. Not with his dedication to the task. Unrelenting attention, over and over. By the time he was done with her she was a happy puddle, stretched out on the king-size mattress in his bedroom.

When her body finally finished shaking, she eased up on her elbows and looked around in astonishment. "When did we move?"

Jim crawled over top of her, crowding her against the mattress. "I think it was about the time you called me a sex god."

She didn't remember the details, but anything was possible...

He lowered himself, covering her in a blanket of heat. The dusting of hair on his chest rubbed her sensitive nipples, and she wondered momentarily if it were possible to die from too much pleasure.

Jim rolled them, easing onto his back and settling her on top of him. "This position will work better."

Lillie pulled her knees up so her sex was pressed over his impressive erection. "I'm not arguing, but I don't think I have the strength left to ride you."

He curled himself up to a sitting position easily, his eight-pack abs bulging against her fingers. "Don't you worry. I've got it under control."

He caught her under the hips and lifted as if she weighed nothing, connecting their mouths as he kissed her, sucking all the air from the room as he pushed her limits. His cock nudged between her folds, the broad head slick with moisture.

He eased her down enough they connected, and a sigh slipped from her lips. "That's so good."

A lift followed by him lowering her farther the next time. Rinse, repeat, until she had completely taken him into her body. She was on the edge of bursting.

She looped her arms around his neck and held her head away so she could gasp. "I'm lightheaded. And so full. Oh my, so so very full."

"Full of cock." Jim's delighted grin lit his face. "You need to work on your dirty talk. You like my cock inside you?"

"It feels so good." She undulated a couple of times before he restrained her.

Her lower lip jutted out before she could stop it.

He nipped at it. "We've only begun."

One hand left her. He teased his fingers down until that wicked thumb of his was back over her clit. She was held tight, unable to do anything except accept the pleasure as he pressed in circles, harder and harder. "Squeeze your pussy around me. Squeeze until you come on my cock."

The flush of heat hit simultaneously—her cheeks, her chest, her clit. It was downright embarrassing the noises escaping her lips, but she couldn't help it anymore. As ordered, she tightened around his cock, and with the pressure building from him rubbing her clit, she had nowhere to escape.

She dug her fingernails into his shoulders as her head fell back, a long cry of pleasure bursting free as he tore another climax from her body.

He took that as the order to move, lifting her hips up before slamming her down. With how sensitive she was, the pounding only made her orgasm continue on, aftershocks rocking her harder than the initial eruption. Again he brought her down, a low growl rising in volume as he lost his rhythm and came, seed filling her, his fingers digging into her butt.

She didn't pass out, didn't lose track of time. Just stayed there, tangled together with his cock deep inside her, her head resting on his chest and her hair draped over his naked body.

Her breathing was still ragged by the time she thought she could move, which was right about the time he picked her up and walked into the bathroom, warm water washing over them as he held her in his arms.

That had been pretty spectacular, and Lillie had absolutely no regrets.

"You're staying the night," Jim informed her.

"I had no intention of going anywhere," she admitted. "But I should warn you, I'm a restless sleeper."

He stroked the hair back off her face and pressed a kiss to her forehead. His words were all tangled up with the low laugh that rumbled from his chest. "What makes you think I intend for us to get any sleep?"

5

———

Jim woke in a cold sweat, his heart pounding and hands fisted in the bed sheets. He looked down to discover he'd shredded not only the quilt and one of the pillows, but deep gouges were visible all the way through the mattress top.

He jerked his head to the left, fearful that in his lurid state he might have hurt Lillie. Usually the presence of a warm, soft body in bed with him was enough to keep the nightmares at bay.

Nothing but a cold pillow and tousled sheets.

He swung his feet to the floor and sat for a moment, slowing his breathing. Head hanging in his hands as he fought for control.

He was glad she hadn't witnessed his attack, but where the hell was she?

The floor underfoot was cold to his bare feet as he made his way to the living area. The curtains at the window were blowing, and he shuffled over to see if she had gone out on the balcony for some strange reason, but no one was there.

The haunting memories that had woken him were

replaced by frustration and confusion, rapidly followed by disgruntlement.

She'd vanished, completely. What the fuck?

She needed to be gone by Friday, anyway, his ambition reminded him.

Shut up. It's only Tuesday, and I was having fun.

Jim stomped to the bedroom and jerked on an outfit, ignoring everything in his rush to get down to the casino. It would be like searching for a needle in a haystack, and he didn't even have his damn phone. He was tempted to ignore Damon's ruling and get someone to drop off his new one immediately.

Best place to start, though, was in the shifter section of the resort. Worst-case scenario, if she wasn't there, and he couldn't find Damon, he'd hire a couple of wolves to track her.

As agitated as he was, Jim couldn't help but glance at his surroundings with a sense of contentment. The glitz and glamour of Vegas might be old hat, but he never got tired of it. Privilege had also made the experience that much more exciting. With his family's reputation, and his money, Jim had discovered all the ins and outs at an early age, including the secret places to go.

Especially the sections of Vegas that catered to the shifter population.

Even at this early hour, the shifter lounge was filled with others of his kind. People with both animal and human sides, who enjoyed life spent part of the time in a furry state. Shifter existence remained mostly hidden from the human world, a task that took a fair bit of secrecy, a healthy dose of luck and some calculated spin doctoring to maintain.

Fortunately, most of the time when there were

incidents, they tended to occur where too much drink on the part of the excited humans could explain away their claims of seeing packs of wolves wandering the halls.

Still was nice to have specific spots they could get away and let their hair down.

He headed toward the bar to ask the man there if he'd seen anyone when one of the majordomos he was familiar with stepped forward, dipping his head politely.

"Mr. Halcyon. I have a message for you, sir."

He slid over a tip before snatching the envelope from the man's hand, turning away to tear it open.

If you're wondering where Goldilocks went, I found her. Figured you might like me to keep an eye on her. ~D

Jim turned over the business card the note was written on to look closer at the name of the shop. It was a modest clothing store in the nearby casino mall. She hadn't had a bag with her last night—and suddenly all sorts of questions rose to mind.

He felt like a shit for not having thought of it sooner. For not asking more about her. She must have a room somewhere in the hotel.

It took a while to reach the shopping plaza, but he found his way unerringly to the store, hanging back in the doorway as he eyed the clothing racks. Comfortable garments, jeans and sweats. He spotted a shirt that would go perfect with her hair, stroking it to make sure the fabric was soft enough for her skin.

"It's not your colour," Damon taunted, stepping beside him.

"Where is she?" Jim demanded.

"I think that's the first time you've ever had a woman

give you the one-night-stand treatment. Don't you usually have to pry them out of bed with trinkets?"

Jim was ready to peel his friend like a banana until he talked. He snapped his head to the side and finally noticed Damon was pointing at a change-room stall.

"How's she doing?"

"I found her hiding in a flower arrangement. She was staring at that banker's check as if it was about to bite her." Damon folded his arms, his face creasing with concern. "She's being secretive about something. I couldn't convince her to grab breakfast with me, although she did agree to let me join her shopping."

"Being shy isn't a crime."

Damon shrugged. "Just making a point. Last night at dinner—did she say anything about herself? Nothing really. I don't know if you two exchanged life stories before, during or after the sex, but the woman is strangely tight-lipped. The entire time I've been around her, the most I've learned is she's a single child, never been to Vegas before, and she wanted to spend some money."

"Not everyone feels the need to spill their entire life stories at first opportunity." Only his friend's comment made Jim consider harder. Nope, he didn't know much about her, but was that lack something he needed to change if she was only a temporary diversion? "She's definitely got enough money to spend."

"She's not keen on lots of people being around," Damon went on quietly. "It took a while before I got her out of her camouflage, and then twice on the walk here, I thought she would bolt."

Oh brother. "I thought you told me to go find someone to take a vacation with."

"I did. I just think you need to enjoy yourself, but stay

alert." His friend's concerned expression twisted into a sneer. "I volunteer to help keep an eye on her."

Damon had a death wish at times. Jim shouldered past him, not bothering to move out of the way, and the contact between their chests sent the other man sprawling to the floor, his good-natured grin still firmly in place.

A mystery was afoot, but Jim had two more pressing issues. He needed to see her to be sure she was okay, and second, he had to keep convincing himself she was just a short-term distraction.

The door to the change room opened a crack, and his anticipation rose as she stepped out.

He wanted to see her dressed in silk, with fabric that would cling to those wonderful curves he had enjoyed so much last night. Something in a deep emerald green, with a plunging neckline worn with dagger-like heels. He wasn't sure if he would cover her with diamonds or find a more modern mineral to grace her neck. Anodized titanium, or even something made from copper.

A quick flash of Lady Luck shot by his vision, replaced with the picture-perfect postcard of a shyly smiling Lillie.

She twirled a lock of hair in her fingers as she blinked innocently. Stone-washed jeans lovingly cupped her butt, a hint of decorative stonework running down one leg. She wore a long-sleeve T-shirt, the green colour he'd imagined her gown should be. The V-neck was cut low enough the smooth upper swells of her cleavage teased him. She held a sturdy leather jacket in her left hand, most of it draped over her shoulder.

"Hey." Her smile brightened.

Jim fought the urge to show his aggravation. She'd crawled out of bed and left him, and that just wasn't right. Instead, he went for control. "I like your outfit."

She twirled, bringing the jacket around to clasp it in front of her with both hands. "Damon said I needed jeans and a jacket. I got some other things already." She flipped a hand toward the cash register. "But this is nice too."

Jim turned an accusing eye on his friend. "Damon said you needed that outfit, did he?"

Damon held up his hands in protest. "Don't go getting the wrong idea. Trust me on this one, bro."

That was asking an awful lot. He closed the gap between them so he could brush a kiss against her lips. "Good morning."

She flushed. "I—"

He tugged the jacket from her fingers and held it out. Lillie turned smoothly, sliding her arms into the sleeves and coming to a stand still as he slipped the fabric over her shoulders and left his hands resting there.

They were facing an enormous gilded mirror, and he leaned over her shoulder to tug the jacket into position so it framed her perfect breasts.

He hummed with approval. "That looks good on you." His lips were directly beside her cheek as he brushed their cheeks together. "Would you like to spend the day with me?"

So much for his declaration of being Mr. Bossy. Yes, he still wanted to be in charge, but ordering this woman around would be like trying to catch a gazelle by shooting off fireworks.

Lillie placed her hands over where he was holding her jacket together under her breasts, his thumbs brushing their soft underside. She didn't say a word for a moment. Just looked at him, glanced momentarily at Damon, then met Jim's gaze and silently nodded.

He wanted to jump up and do a backflip, but that

wouldn't have been very dignified. "Anything special you want to do?"

Lillie turned excitedly. "Yes. There's a show I want to get tickets for, and there's a restaurant that got a super review, and I want to learn to dance."

Jim smiled and nodded all the way up to the last one.

"Oh, and Damon said he had something planned for part of the day too."

Jim turned to examine his friend. "Damon seems full of good ideas today, doesn't he?"

The wolf only grinned, stepping well out of Jim's arm reach. "Wow, look at the time. I have somewhere I have to be."

"Strange, but convenient." Jim's possessiveness was well satisfied as Lillie snuck her fingers into his. The warm touch of her small hand settled him.

"How about this?" Damon looked directly at Lillie. "You guys have fun for the morning, set up whatever show you want to see tonight, and after lunch, meet me in the shifter lounge. Then we can do that fun thing I planned."

No way could Jim protest when Lillie bounced on her heels with excitement. "That sounds wonderful. Thank you, Damon."

"Yeah, Damon, that sounds just peachy keen."

His friend gloated with maximum gloatingness. "I'll see you there."

"Wait." Lillie stepped forward, her arm stretching behind her as Jim refused to release her fingers. She glanced at their locked hands, a frown building on her forehead, and he reluctantly set her free. She turned back to the wolf, her chin tucked down but her voice crystal clear. "You were very kind to me this morning. Thank you."

"No problem, darlin'. You're very easy to be kind to."

Damon pretended to tip a hat then turned on his heel and left.

Jim glared after him. The only thing remotely country about his friend was the barbeque sauce he put on his burgers.

Then Lillie caught his hand, pulling him toward the register, and that small touch was enough to settle his frustrations. "I need to pay for my things, then maybe we can look at the shows."

THEY WERE BACK in the shifter lounge, tickets in her pocket for a performance of Cirque de Soleil. The brand-new bag Jim had insisted on buying her was tucked safely into a backroom, guarded by a smiling mink shifter who'd backed off flirting with her as Jim hovered protectively.

She wondered briefly why she was still with him. What she should have done that morning was switched to another hotel, or at least gone back to her hotel room and stayed far away from the temptation of Jim.

In fact, that had been her intention when she snuck out of the room, but within moments of reaching the lobby, she'd been overwhelmed with the arrival of a group of Japanese tourists and the sheer number of bodies milling about.

Her hiding spot had been discovered within minutes by Damon. And while she wasn't as comfortable with him as Jim, the protection he offered was too soothing to turn down.

Her debate had continued right up until Jim asked her to spend the day with him. Now that she'd actually experienced Vegas, she knew she had little chance of managing everything on her short-term bucket list on her own.

There really was no downside to spending more time with him. He was gentle, which she appreciated. Even as he led her to the back of the lounge, his broad body created a wall between her and the rest of the shifters.

The strong hand on her back guiding and protecting.

If it came down to it, she could find a way to defend herself, but it was nice to allow him the task.

"Do you know what Damon has planned?" she asked.

"Not entirely, but if I have to guess, I'd imagine from the outfit he got you to buy, and our plans for the end of the week, we might be going for a ride."

Lillie glanced up. "What are you doing at the end of the week?"

"Long-standing bet. It's something Damon and I started years ago. Friday we'll be taking off for the hills for a bit." He held her close, pausing to allow a large party to pass.

She breathed a sigh of relief. That worked well with her plans. Now she could relax and not have to worry about having to sneak away. Friday would be perfect for the next stage in her journey.

Then the other part of what he'd said struck. "A ride. Like, horses?"

Damon waved to them from the corner of the room, and they headed in his direction. "Motorcycles," Jim informed her.

The idea sounded fabulous, but she was uncomfortable about inviting herself along. Still, she kept quiet. There would be time to protest later if necessary.

The wolf shifter smacked Jim on the shoulder in greeting, reaching out to take Lillie's hand and pull her close enough he could drop a kiss on her cheek. "Glad to see you could make it."

Jim reclaimed her, tucking her against his side and growling lightly.

Damon raised a brow. "Just being friendly."

She couldn't restrain the words from popping free. "I would hate to see how you'd react to someone who wasn't a friend giving me a kiss."

Both men offered her horrified looks. Damon, as if he'd just witnessed a mauling, and Jim, as if he'd just torn someone apart. It didn't freak her out nearly as much as it should have. They were shifters, or more accurately they were shifter *males*.

There was a certain predictability built into such beasts.

...but it was time to change the subject.

Lillie bumped her enthusiasm up to five hundred, turning to the table and the piles of clothing stacked on it. "Looks as if you did some shopping of your own."

Damon nodded. "Some things are necessary to make a great idea even greater."

The grizzly shifter at her side shuffled forward and poked one of the piles. "Why don't I trust you?"

"Because you know me," Damon teased. "But this time, what you see is what you get. I thought if we were going to do a bike race for the challenge, we should fully enjoy the moment."

"Practice saying it. Jim won. Jim won. Jim won."

His friend snickered, pushing one pile to the side as he dropped a wink at Lillie. "Sometimes my friend has delusions of grandeur."

"Only sometimes?" Lillie deadpanned, laughing as Jim's fingers danced on her waist, tickling her.

Damon's laugh echoed in the room. "I like you." He

motioned to Jim. "Shut up and change." He slipped off his jacket and shirt, reaching into his pile for a sky-blue bundle of fabric.

Lillie smiled. It wasn't that she considered Damon particularly vain, but he'd purchased a shirt in a colour exactly matching his eyes. Jim noticed as well, and they exchanged amused glances.

She peeked at the clothing Jim was sorting through, but instead of dark brown there was a black T-shirt.

"Do I get to keep my underwear?" Jim jibed.

A low chuckle escaped Damon. "We're not discussing boxers versus briefs versus commando. We had that conversation when we were twelve. Once a lifetime is enough."

A couple of wolves in their animal form trotted past as the guys changed. Lillie leaned back on a nearby table and didn't bother to hide her admiration.

By shifter standards, going down to skin wasn't considered dirty. They needed to be naked when they shifted. That didn't lower her appreciation for the eye candy on display. Both of them, Damon's leaner wolf physique, Jim's bulkier overall mass.

Damon finally pulled on his jacket and held out his arms, rotating slowly. "So, what do you think?"

Faded jeans, that killer T-shirt nicely showcasing the muscles he'd forced the material over, all of it topped with a leather jacket that had a massive wolf head on the back and *Leader of the Pack* emblazoned over it.

Lillie nodded her approval. "I like."

Jim flipped his jacket over, and Lillie left her perch to peek around him, clinging to his arms. His logo was an enormous bear head, definitely a grizzly, and the banner said *Don't Miss The Branch.*

She puzzled for a moment before the children's song popped into her head, threatening to become an unending earworm.

God, that was hysterical.

"I love it."

Jim grunted lightly. "At least the bastard didn't use teddy bears like he did before."

"I swear the guy at the print shop had the biggest trouble understanding what I wanted. And he wanted me to give you his name."

A frown crossed Jim's face. "Why?"

Damon cleared his throat. "He says he loves bears."

"He didn't know we were shifters, did he?" Jim's eyes widened with understanding the same moment it hit Lillie.

Oh my. "You're not hairy enough to be that kind of bear."

Oops.

Lillie covered her mouth with her hand even as Damon lost his serious expression and burst into peals of laughter.

Jim shook his head. "Glad I could be of entertainment. Yeah, not enough fur in human form, and I don't swing that way, so the poor guy will have to keep on dreaming."

His friend wiped his eyes, taking a deep breath and letting it out slowly. "I tell you, keeping a straight face was damn hard."

"I bet it destroyed you," Jim drawled.

"I love both your outfits, and you look great," Lillie offered.

Jim nodded his agreement. "I don't know who you killed to get the outfits, but I'm keeping mine. We only need bikes to complete the set."

"Now that you mention it..." Damon looked her over

carefully, nodding as she pulled on her leather jacket. "I think we're ready."

He led them out the nearby exit door to where two beautiful motorcycles stood waiting.

"Sweet." Lillie walked around them, running her hand over the shiny metal and soft black leather. "Harleys?"

"Mine is," Damon confirmed, patting one of the bikes. He pointed at the other one that Jim was already throwing a leg over. "That's a Ducati. Jim has more expensive tastes than I do. I had to splurge for the fancy Italian job for him."

"My friend, I forgive you for every sin you've ever committed against me." Jim ran his hands over the handlebars, shaking his head slightly as he admired the bike. "Well, except for the incident when we were seven. That one I will hate you for until my dying day."

Damon pulled a helmet off his bike, pointing to the back of Jim's. "I don't know why you insist that was my fault. Bears swim, wolves swim. How was I supposed to know not all honey badgers like to swim?"

"You weren't the one she climbed on top of," Jim growled.

Lillie was thrilled to see a helmet for her as well, but she waited until Jim handed it to her, suddenly apprehensive to come between the two old friends. "I don't have to join you. This is something special for you and—"

"Put on your helmet and get your butt on the bike," Jim ordered. Then his stern expression softened. "As long as you're comfortable. You're not afraid, are you?"

She flushed slightly at exactly how comfortable she was. "Not if you're driving."

His nod of approval sent warm tingles all over her.

Damon held his helmet before him, his long limbs already draped over his bike. "That settles it. Let's take them out and see what they can do." He plopped his helmet over his blond hair and put his hands to the controls.

Before she was in position, Damon was gone, tires spinning on the pavement as he took off in a squeal of smoke and noise.

She tightened the strap under her chin. "I'm not slowing you down, am I?"

Jim shook his head, lifting her into position behind him. He pulled her close, her thighs nestled against his, warm and intimate and completely safe as she wrapped her arms around his torso and held on tight. He took off slower than Damon, but the wind whistled past and Lillie found she was wearing a wide, goofy grin.

Her last hurrah was turning out to be one of the best experiences of her life.

6

They headed north on the highway, then off on a secondary road into the mountains. It hadn't taken long for Jim to catch up with Damon, and they rode side by side, easing around corners as the landscape changed, trees beginning to thicken as they gained elevation.

A sign flashed past informing them they were headed toward Mount Charleston. This area was familiar territory as well. Jim and Damon had played in the park before, but it was nice to be able to look forward to showing Lillie something different.

And he appreciated Damon hadn't taken them out for hours. Jim had worked Lillie over pretty hard last night, and the fifty minutes it would take to get to the parking lot at the trailhead was more than enough.

She leaned against his back, hands locked around his waist. Every time there was the slightest bump in the road, her grip rubbed him and set his body on fire.

The parking lot was empty when they got there. Lillie pulled off her helmet, her expression one of wonder as she looked around. "Okay, I confess. This is much more my speed than the casino floors."

Damon hung his helmet on the handlebars, pulling off his jacket. "Why did you decide to come to Vegas if you're not comfortable around crowds?"

For a second it seemed as if she was actually going to answer the question, and then that barrier went up. She hesitated long enough Jim was sure she was debating how much truth to include in her story.

"I only had a few choices, and I always wanted to see Vegas." She turned her back on them, pacing toward the wide map erected at the trailhead.

Damon gave Jim a pointed look, as in *See? She's keeping secrets.* And yet, as long as they weren't terrible secrets, who was he to judge?

He changed the subject before Damon could say anything out loud. "We have time for a bit of a stroll."

His friend removed his shirt, gesturing toward the box at the side of the trail. "Best invention ever."

Lillie poked her head around the side of the map. "A food cache?"

"We put our clothes in them so no one steals our stuff while we go for a walk in our fur." Jim held out his hand to her. "I donated this one so we'd have a safe place to put things."

"What he's not telling you is before we had this here, someone once absconded with everything but our shoes. It made for an interesting trip back to town." Damon winked, and she laughed.

Jim inclined his head toward the trail. "Did you want to shift for a while? I promise it's safe. No one's going to get upset even if we are spotted."

Her smile was full of mischief. "You're sure no one will

think twice about seeing a grizzly, a black bear and a wolf hanging out together for the day?"

Damon was already down to skin, stuffing his boots into the square metal box. "That's nothing. I came here once with a few friends—a cougar, a lion, a couple more—and we were playing tag. Someone caught a satellite shot of the moment when the mink was chasing us all."

Her lips curled happily. "I'd love to walk for a while."

Jim knew it wasn't necessary, not for Lillie's sake, but for his own peace of mind he kept himself between her and his best friend as they stripped. He accepted her pile of clothing, letting his gaze drift over her creamy skin, the sunlight bouncing off her curves.

She shook a finger at him. "I recognize that expression. I thought you said you wanted to go for a ramble, not a tumble."

"One, and then the other," he compromised.

She still wore her smile as she shifted, her petite human body transforming into the daintiest black bear he'd ever seen. Jim paced forward, squatting down to gaze into her eyes as he stroked her head. "Look at you. I could eat you up in one bite," he teased.

Lillie snapped at him before sitting back on her haunches, tilting her head to the side in the most adorable way.

Jim tucked their clothing into the safe box and locked it firmly. Then he joined her, going down by her side. "How are you doing, sweetie?"

Damon trotted up beside him, the silver wolf with black markings on his shoulders wagging his tail excitedly, typical enthusiasm pouring from his friend. Lillie wiggled slightly, then leaned forward and touched her nose to Damon's. The wolf responded playfully, bouncing on his front paws from crouch to crouch, moving side to side, ready to play.

Jim placed his hand against Damon's shoulder and shoved him hard enough to send the wolf off balance. "Stop flirting," he commanded.

Damon kept rolling until he regained his feet, his teeth showing as he laughed.

Jim turned his attention back on Lillie. "No problems meeting Damon's wolf?"

She shook her head before rising to her feet and closing in on him. He stayed still and allowed her to circle him, then she stood patiently, waiting.

Only one way to find out if she could handle him. Jim shifted, the moment of change between the human and the animal rushing over him with a sweet, sensual tease. He was glad the stories were wrong. There was no painful grinding of limbs as their bones rearranged themselves. Whatever it was that allowed them to shift felt damn good.

Looking at the world with his adjusted vision was amazing as always. The sounds around him were just as intense as in his human, but they somehow made more sense when he was in animal form. Same thing for the scents—growing richer and clearer with every breath he took.

Lillie still waited for him, and he moved in closer, slowly rubbing their shoulders together. She didn't seem to mind. In fact, she pushed back before prancing away nearly as playfully as Damon.

Thank goodness. He had hoped she would trust him, but he knew his bear was a big brute. He'd frightened other shifters, even ones who weren't nearly as timid as her to begin with.

She darted off down the trail and around the trees,

leaving the packed gravel and cutting across country toward the nearby ridge. Damon didn't wait for the signal to run, the three of them moving into the wilderness easily as the sunshine lit the hillside.

No matter how civilized shifters were, the mix of human and animal meant there was a part inside that would always crave the wilderness. This was the reason, even though Jim hated the thought of heading to the home he had in the north, he couldn't give it up.

Running with the others along the ridge gave him time to consider. He'd been going on sheer will power for the last year, hiding from the pain of his loss.

Money couldn't fix everything.

And while his parents and he had been trapped in a cave-in, it wasn't the darkness that left him waking in a cold sweat. It was the loss of family and connection. Bears didn't tend to congregate often in the first place. Hell, they were such loners they'd even put conventions in place to arrange marriages between compatible individuals to ensure bear shifters didn't vanish altogether.

His enjoyment of being around others was rare, and he truly believed only his friendship with Damon had helped him get through those early months of despair.

He still hadn't returned to the home being built outside of Whitehorse. The last time he'd been there was with his parents, as he showed them the plans for the mansion. They'd approved of his choices—admired his successes, and teased him mercilessly about how big the place was, and how many children he'd have to have to fill the empty rooms.

And now they were gone.

A long, low howl echoed off the hills. Damon, letting loose a cry. His tone was somewhere between sheer joy and utter sadness, and Jim wondered again at the depths of his joking friend. The things that burdened Damon were so tightly wrapped up even Jim couldn't pry the chains apart.

He rambled to a stop beside his friend, bumping the wolf with his hip. Damon only howled louder, but this time a hint of laughter returned to the sound.

Jim turned his attention to his mysterious woman. As a diversion, she'd been everything he could have hoped for and then some. He was already looking forward to spending the evening with her, even if that meant taking in a show instead of taking her straight to bed.

He wasn't sure if it was selfishness on his part, or if he was being kind by not delving deeper into her secrets.

The only thing he knew for sure? He was damn glad he'd met her.

IT HAD BEEN the perfect day, Lillie decided. A bit of everything—from shopping, to the trip to the mountains, to the enormous pile of In-and-Out Burgers they consumed.

Add in the expression on the counter girl's face as she'd taken their order for twenty-five burgers and eight orders of fries—hysterical. Especially when Damon had to go back and order a couple more, complaining he was still hungry.

Buzzzzzzz.

Lillie dried her hands on the towel, checking her texts as she left the restaurant bathroom.

Check-in time

Lillie wrote rapidly. *Still alive. Having fun. No time to talk—going to show*

Still flinging?

Yes. Gotta run

<3

The brief contact reassured her. Addie was there if needed, but so far, everything was going marvelously.

All the way up to, and including, getting ready for their show.

Fingers trailed over her shoulder as she put the final touches on her makeup.

"Did you buy this today? It looks great." Jim pressed his lips to her skin and sent goose bumps rising.

Lillie hesitated. She didn't want to tell him too much, but she didn't want to lie either. "No, I had this with me."

He glanced in the mirror, adjusting his tie as he spoke. "Oh, in the bag you picked up from the valet." He was deliberately not looking directly at her, she could tell. "I meant to mention. If you have a room booked for tomorrow night, why don't you go ahead and cancel it. May as well save the money."

Her cheeks were flushed. "I didn't want to assume. I mean, I know you guys are taking off on Friday, but I'd like to stay with you, only any time if you don't want me around anymore you have to let me know—"

He caught her gaze in the mirror and held her pinned in place with that alone. He didn't speak for long enough she began to get squirrelly.

When he finally did say something, it was in a low, careful tone of voice. "I'm not making any demands. No expectations. You're welcome to stay with me, that's all I was saying."

She nodded vigorously then turned away, cursing her situation.

"Did you have any other bags you need to rescue?" Jim asked. "I won't ask any questions, just letting you know you can tuck them in a corner here so they're safe."

He was getting closer to discovering the truth every moment, and Lillie's confidence wavered.

Maybe this wasn't a great idea, hanging out with a man like Jim. He inspired her confidence and made it all too tempting to spill the beans. And yet, it wasn't as if she were headed into a terrible situation. She was okay with what her future held.

Time to focus on the shining moments she had in the here and now. "My things are in storage. They'll be okay until I go get them."

Thank goodness, he changed the topic, dropping it completely as he brought her hand to his knuckles to make her body light up with desire.

"We're sitting in a more private section for the show," he informed her as they skipped the main entrance, and a side door opened before them. Uniformed servants slid out of sight as he walked her forward. "I thought it would make it easier for you to not have to deal with the crowds."

"I'm getting more used to them," she insisted, squeezing her arms as he guided her toward a loveseat in a private alcove. "And it's easier when I'm with you. I feel safe."

She didn't get a chance to admire their surroundings, because the instant they were both seated, Jim leaned over and kissed her. She responded eagerly, hungry for more of his touch. He'd been a complete gentleman the entire afternoon, stealing small caresses but in a way that she didn't feel pawed or owned.

She felt cared for. Valued.

So as they waited for the show to start, Lillie curled her fingers into his hair and soaked in the pleasure he offered. And when the lights went down and the curtain went up, she was sad all she had was his hand in hers.

Lillie snuggled against his side, pressing her palm to his

chest as her gaze remained glued to the stage. He laid his hand over hers, outlining her fingers one at a time. A lovely caress that rooted her in place and let her relax from the small bit of tension that had come from having all those people around them.

She caught herself stroking him, and as the music rose in the performance, a contented rumble escaped from the man beside her.

"You keep doing that, and I'll think you want me to pet you as well," he warned, his lips brushing her ear.

Oh. Well now.

Temptation waved a set of pom-poms, and suddenly far more important than any of the acrobatics happening before her was discovering exactly what type of petting Jim had in mind.

She stroked in circles, twirling her fingers until she discovered his nipple under the dress shirt. She kicked off her shoes and adjusted her legs so she could reach better, undoing the center button on his shirt and slipping her hand under the fabric.

This time when she touched him she had fingers to bare skin. Brushing over the wiry hair on his chest to tease him, tweaking the flat disk of his nipple until he rumbled.

Up on the stage the dancing grew wilder, the music a heavy drumbeat, and her courage rose. Lillie made quick work of his next two buttons, leaving his collar and tie in place, his shirttails still tucked in, but now she had room to stroke and caress his muscular abdomen. To drag her nails over his skin.

What she really wanted was to undo his zipper and pull his cock free.

And then the realization hit—why not?

He hissed as she tugged at the metal tab holding back

the solid rock in his pants. But he didn't stop her. Not then, and not when she reached in and wrapped her fingers around the thick heat she found.

It was dark enough around them she didn't think anyone could see what she was doing, even if they could pry their eyes away from the stage.

Jim shrugged out of his suit jacket and tossed it casually over his lap, easing his hips forward on the couch and laying his head on the backrest.

Lillie lifted onto her knees far enough to press her lips to his cheek. "Okay?"

Luckily something happened on stage at the same moment he let out a loud *Ha*, his exclamation buried under the applause and *ooooohs* and *ahhhhhs*.

"Tell me every dirty thing you want me to do to you," Jim growled.

Lillie sucked in a quick breath. She stroked her palm over the soft head of his cock, spreading the moisture she found. "Right now?"

"Right now," he whispered. "As long as you keep talking, I'll let you keep stroking me. Let's see who can last longer."

As a challenge, something seemed off. "You're going to come if I keep touching you."

Another loud burst of applause from the audience.

"Tell me, sweetheart," he insisted. "Or do you want me to touch you? Find a place where anyone could watch us, and for me to put my fingers on your pretty pussy?"

Lillie swallowed hard. "Um...no."

She quickly thought of things she wanted to tell him, because if he kept talking? It didn't matter whether he was touching her or not, she would be squirming so hard someone would figure out what was going on.

"I like you touching me," she confessed, "but not where anyone can see us. I think it would be fun to be in total darkness. Not knowing where you would touch me next." She pulled his cock free and stroked, rolling her hand up the length slowly.

He caught her wrist and brought her fingers to his mouth, licking her palm before replacing it around his erection. This time her hand slid smoother, and she resumed the slow, steady pulse.

"I'd like to try sex in the dark," she stated firmly. "Not as if you're chasing me, because I might get scared. But more like a treasure hunt. You'd have to touch me slowly, learning what I felt like since you wouldn't be able to see me."

Just like now, as she learned what he felt like. Her gaze fixed on stage as she concentrated on the subtle changes in his body on every rise and fall of her fist over his cock.

"And in the shower. Somewhere wet, although I don't think a Jacuzzi is a good idea because it might be too hot, but a shower would be neat. Moisture would run down your body, and I'd lick it away. And you could rub us together, so slippery and warm that when you push into me it would be as if our entire bodies were connected."

His cock jerked in her hand, more than slick enough now as precome spilled from the tip and over her palm. He covered her hand with his own, increasing the pressure and speed.

The challenge wasn't over. Lillie squared her mental shoulders and went for broke. "But the one I want the most is from behind. Your big, strong body over top of me, your arms caging me in, but protecting me. I can feel you touching every part of my back—your groin tight to my butt. You would be so hard against me, and then you'd reach around and play with me. My breasts, between my legs..."

She shivered, her rhythm over his erection faltering as the images she described made her body ache. He kept the pace going, but now it was ninety percent his effort moving her hand over him as she concentrated on finishing.

"You'd rock between my legs—"

"My cock," Jim demanded in a low growl as a clash of cymbals went off, and a performer soared across the open air. "*Say it.* Say you want my *cock* between your legs."

"Yes." Her breathing stuttered, increasing in tempo along with the music rising around them as the first act built to its stunning finale. "I want your...*cock*...between my legs, pumping back and forth. I can feel it rubbing over my... pussy. Getting you all wet, until you stop teasing and push into me all at once. Thick and hot and oh-so-good."

He made a noise in his throat.

She probably sounded as hoarse as him.

"And then you...fuck me. Hard."

"*Lillie*..." He closed his eyes, scrambling under the coat with his left hand. His fingers closed over hers as a stream of heat escaped, making her stickier as together they pulled another rasping gasp from him.

She squeezed her legs together, attempting to calm her breathing as the room exploded with shouts and bangs, the concluding crescendo of the first performance synchronizing with the final jerks of his climax.

A smile stretched her lips. Even turned on and aching, she had never felt more satisfied. At least, not until he stole her away during the third act, took her back to his suite and proceeded to do everything she'd suggested.

All night long.

7

One minute she was curled up in his arms, the next there was a heavy weight on his chest and he was gasping for air.

Jim shoved off the sheets, relieved to see he'd managed to avoid shredding them this time. Only familiar thing? Lillie was gone, and gone for long enough her spot was cool to the touch.

How did she manage to get out of bed without him noticing?

Thankfully, this time when he stomped into the living room, she was sitting there, a computer open on the coffee table as she bounced her head in time with a quietly playing music video.

His gaze darted to the corner of the room. Suitcases were stacked neatly in the corner, each large enough for an extended trip. Good-quality fabric, and Jim tucked the information away for future consideration. He was more interested in making sure she was happy for the time they got to be together.

It was only right.

She glanced up as he paced forward, that shy smile spreading over her face as she rose. "Hey. You're finally awake, sleepyhead."

He glanced at the clock. "It's only seven a.m."

"Half the day is practically gone." She tucked herself against him, curling her arms around his back and lifting her face to be kissed. He had no objections whatsoever, falling into her soft touch for a couple of moments.

When she stepped away, he took a closer look to see what she was wearing. "You snuck into my wardrobe."

Lillie glanced down at the plain white shirt she wore, the tails hanging past her knees. A mischievous smile greeted him as she headed toward the kitchen. "Would you like some coffee? I made a pot."

"You could have called for butler service, you know." Trailing after her was only logical, since it meant he got to look at her legs. "We're getting you a different sleep shirt. That one covers too much of your ass."

She paused in the middle of pouring him a coffee. "But if I take off the shirt, we'll never leave the suite."

Jim thought about her comment for a good long time— all the way until he took his first sip of coffee. "Nope. Just can't see the trouble in that."

Lillie poked his side gently as she passed him, curling her fingers around his hip. "Well, I have plans for the day. And if you want, you can come along, but otherwise I'll meet you for dinner. It's up to you."

She wasn't getting out of his sight. Not only because she still had all that extra cash on her, but because—

Just because.

It's Wednesday already, dude. Time's a ticking.

Shut up. It's only Wednesday.

"What are your plans?" He settled beside her on the

couch, his legs on either side of her body as she sat on the floor and opened a website.

"Look." She tapped on the screen. "I already contacted them, and there's a class at ten, so there's time for breakfast before we go. Before I go. Whatever."

Jim looked closer at the website, trailing his fingers through her hair as he examined the pictures. She hummed happily as he stroked the long tresses back over her shoulder and into a bundle. "Dance lessons. You mentioned that yesterday. Don't they have lessons where you come from?"

She stiffened, and he pressed his fingers to her scalp, rubbing until her body relaxed. "Not this kind of dancing."

He was far more interested in touching her than examining the details on the screen. "You have a hairbrush with you?" he asked.

She uncurled herself from the floor and headed to one of the smaller suitcases, opening the side pouch and pulling out a bristly object. "I think I have a bunch of knots," she warned.

"Probably," he said, resettling her between his knees. "You should have grabbed your brush sooner, but I'll take care of you."

He worked slowly, one section at a time, holding the molten mass in his hand and carefully working out each tangle. She leaned on his legs, her arms curled around his shins as she allowed him to move her head as he needed. Brush after brush, the small tangles pulled to shimmering lines of copper, until the morning sunlight burst in the window. Then he was brushing a fistful of sunbeams, sparkling jewels tangling around his fingers as he worked the bristles through again and again.

Sensual, and yet not. After all the sexual fun they'd experienced, in some ways this moment felt the most intimate. They were quiet together, no words needed as he cared for her and she trusted him.

When she sighed happily, closing the cover on her computer, Jim pulled her into his lap. Lillie tucked herself against his chest.

"I really am having the most marvelous time," she confessed. "But then I start to feel guilty because we're just having a fling, and I know you didn't want anything long-term, and neither do I, but I still feel guilty even though it's on my bucket list and—"

"Hush." He pressed a finger over her lips and let out a deep contented sigh of his own. "No guilt necessary. I've been enjoying myself too. It's been a long time since I simply played, instead of working. I should be thanking you for giving up so much of your vacation time to accommodate me."

She wrinkled her nose. "It's not really a vacation—"

The elevator buzzed. The door slid open, and Damon wandered in. "Top of the morning to you, mates. Are y'all ready for some crackin' fine adventures on this bonny day?"

It was his own fault for giving the bastard a pass card for the elevator in the first place. Jim was ready to revoke Damon's best-friend status. He stretched his arm over the couch and twisted to watch his friend approach. "Did I invite you?"

Damon shook his head. "If I waited for an invitation, I'd never get asked up here. I'm no dummy." He dropped into the chair opposite the couch. "Morning, Lillie. Sleep well?"

Lillie wiggled out of Jim's lap, crossing her knees carefully as she settled at his side. "Of course. Thank you for asking."

Damon's gaze dropped over her, taking in the shirt and

her bare legs. His grin faded slightly, but only Jim who knew him so well would've noticed.

Something was wrong.

Then the wolf's charms-their-panties-off smile returned. "Neither of you are ready for breakfast. Why don't you go get dressed, Lillie? I need to chat with the Griz-Man for a mo."

"Sure," she said willingly, popping up from his side.

Jim caught her around the waist and sent her tumbling back into his lap. "You didn't say goodbye," he scolded.

Her eyes sparkled as she pressed her lips to his cheek. "Thank you for brushing my hair. And thank you for the shirt."

Her lips moved along his cheek to touch the corner of his mouth, a light touch like a butterfly's wings before she pulled away, off his lap, and slipped back into his bedroom.

He was still staring after her when Damon cleared his throat before speaking quietly enough Lillie couldn't overhear.

"Two nights in a row? Aren't you ready to trade her in for a new model?"

Jim glared at his friend. "Make up your mind. Didn't you say something about how I should take time off, find someone to screw? I do believe that's what you said."

"It was, and it is." Damon crossed his arms, concern painting his expression. "And I know you enjoy the ladies. Only something seems different this time. You just seem to be getting in really deep, really fast."

Jim couldn't stop it. A chuckle burst free.

Damon twirled a cushion across the room at him. "And you say I have a dirty mind."

"You do," confirmed Jim. "Why are you so tangled up about me finding someone who scratches my itch?"

"Did she tell you anything more about where she came from? Or why she's here?"

Jim rolled his eyes. "Why? Do you think she's an ax murderer in disguise or something?"

"She could be. You have no way of knowing."

"Maybe I should go through her luggage and see how many poisoned blades she's carrying." Jim tossed a hand toward the luggage in the corner.

Damon's eyes widened. "Maybe you should..."

"Stop right there."

His friend froze in the middle of rising to his feet in an awkwardly tilted squat position.

Jim glared evilly. "Don't touch her things. No, I haven't tried to dig any more information out of her, because frankly, it's none of my business. We're having a good time together for a few days, and come Friday, she's heading her direction and you and I are heading to the hills. Comprendo?"

A long pause followed as Damon switched to pacing the room. "I think you need to be smart about this."

"I understand," Jim insisted. "And your heart is in a good place, but your head is somewhere else. She's here for a good time. I'm having a *really* good time—enough said. Thank you for your concern."

"Message received, loud and clear. I won't say another word on the matter." Damon rested his hands on the back of the couch and leaned forward. "Out of curiosity... Do you still have the coin?"

Oh, for fuck's sake.

Jim got to his feet and headed to the bureau in front of the window. He hauled open the middle drawer more violently than he needed to, reaching in and pulling out Lady Luck from where Damon had left it the other day. He thrust his hand into the air, the coin easily visible. "Satisfied?" he demanded, still speaking softly. "Or did you want to test it for authenticity? Because, you know, maybe sometime in the five minutes she and I haven't been together here in the apartment, she managed to make an exact copy from strands of her hair, and that's what I'm holding."

He shook the plastic case, the coin rattling loudly.

"All I'm saying," Damien whispered back as he walked toward him, "is if the shoe were on the other foot, you'd be warning me to keep my head. There's something not right here."

"And this is your wolfie senses speaking?"

"Maybe," Damon bit out before softening his tone. "Maybe it's that I'm a friend, and I don't want to see you hurt."

Jim breathed slowly, letting his frustration ride out along with his exhale. He closed the distance between himself and his friend. "Tell you what." He offered Lady Luck to Damon. "This needs to be given to the judge anyway. Why don't you arrange that this morning—plus set up the rules of engagement. Where we report in, what we bring to prove we completed the challenge—all that shit. Do it today, and that's one less thing for us to worry about."

"No problem. Anything for you." Damon took the coin with reverence, as if being offered something precious. He offered Jim a wry smile. "Sorry for being a jackass. I don't know why I'm itchy about her."

Jim pressed his hands to Damon's shoulders and held on tight. "I appreciate your concern, more than you know. You've been a rock in my life, Damon, and I don't tell you often enough. Things really are okay."

Damon patted him on the back, and Jim gave him an

extra squeeze, and they ended up doing that guy thing where you almost pound each other into the floor rather than actually give each other a hug.

As close to saying *I love you* as two best friends could, or ever would.

~

"ARE you sure there's enough material in this outfit I won't get arrested for indecent exposure?"

The woman helping Lillie into her dance costume cracked her bubble gum loudly, her bright red lipstick contrasting sharply with her sparkling white teeth. "Oh, you look just perfect, darlin'. You wait till you try those moves you practiced in the studio out there on stage."

A shiver rolled over Lillie's skin. "There's no real audience, right?" she asked for the fifth time.

"Of course not. You're nowhere near performance ready, but it's a good thing to try your moves on the stage for fun. See if you learned enough to be able to go and do some sexy dancing for that someone special."

Sylvia winked as she adjusted the miniscule bra over Lillie's breasts, pulling the strategically placed tassels into tangle-free lines. "And that someone special out there, you won't be able to see, not really. We turn on spotlights the same as you have on a stage. No, just do the routine we taught you, and if you have any trouble you peek up at the right corner where there's a video playing to remind you."

Lillie took a deep breath. "It has been fun."

"Of course it has." Sylvia smoothed the line of the barely there shorts Lillie wore. "Not only am I a fabulous instructor, this is all about getting in touch with your inner sensual beast."

It didn't seem right to giggle.

This was definitely a story she would share with Addie. Her friend would have gotten a kick out of seeing her shy little Lillie up on the stage.

"Right through there, and you can use the pole on the left. We'll have the music start once you're in place, and remember there's nothing you can't do in this routine. This is about having fun and celebrating your sexuality. Let your inner goddess pour out of you as you celebrate being a woman."

Lillie had an attack of the giggles she fought valiantly to keep under control.

While she liked her sexuality, she didn't tend to talk about it in those terms. Walking out onto the wooden stage, her high-heel boots clicking against the surface, she was more worried about keeping her balance than strutting her stuff.

Still, the dance lessons had been a blast. The spotlights on her blocked the entire view of the audience, and when another set turned on, this time with a red glow, Lillie let herself fall into the fantasy.

She was two days away from having to meet her destiny. Two more days to be wild-and-free Lillie with the sexy Jim who sat in the empty auditorium watching her.

Even that thought couldn't make her nervous as she wrapped her right hand around the pole and stood beside it. Chin lifted high, legs spread shoulder-width apart, she stared straight ahead like Sylvia had taught her and pretended no one was around.

No one who mattered but herself...*and Jim.*

The music began. Slow and bluesy, with lots of low horn tones that reverberated off the high ceiling of the stage. Lillie worked through the first moves Sylvia had demonstrated, stepping around the pole and concentrating as she wiggled her hips and struck different poses.

But after the first few moments, it was less about exactly duplicating what she'd been taught as she slipped into a happy zone, pulsing to the beat of the music with more than one body part at a time.

She squatted low then spun around the pole, extending her legs and coming back up to vertical with her body close enough she made contact with the cool metal. She added a body arch. Her long hair fell loose over her shoulders as she danced, brushing her skin with a sensual tease.

The lights grew hotter, and the pole warmed under her hands. Now she was glad her outfit had so little material because she was working up a sweat, her feet staying within a one-foot radius of the solid metal shaft.

Everything centered on the pole.

She wrapped one leg around it, dragging her hands up to her breasts and beyond until she was reaching overhead, arched back and held only by the single connection point.

Even with the volume of music pulsing around her, she swore she heard a growl from the audience.

The heat in the room shot sky high.

Jim.

He was out there. And no matter what Sylvia had said about this being a dance for Lillie to celebrate her sexuality, Lillie knew the truth. This was also a dance for him.

A thank-you for having taken the time to protect her and ease her fears. Her entire trip could have turned out so differently. Addie was right about that, and it was only fool's luck Lillie hadn't ended up in dire straits.

So she hauled herself back to vertical as she lowered her gaze, guessing where he might be. She loosened another snap on her bra and let more of her breasts show.

The final beats of the song were drawing near, and Lillie put her heart and soul into her motions. Dancing for herself, yes, but dancing for him as well.

When the music stopped and the lights clicked off, Lillie's heart continued to pound, and she struggled to catch her breath.

No wild applause greeted her from the audience, no catcalls or whistles. In fact, it was eerily silent considering she was certain she'd heard Jim before.

She was too invigorated by her successful venture to be disappointed for long, and she turned to the back of the room, heading for the faint crack of light showing the way off the stage.

That had been absolutely amazing.

She pushed through the curtain, and her feet left the floor.

"You did that on purpose," Jim rumbled, carrying her rapidly from the stage area and down a dark hall. "You didn't tell me what kind of dance you were doing. I sat there in the dark thinking you were going to come out and sashay yourself across the stage, or do a cancan, or some such nonsense. But no, you decided to drive me fucking crazy."

Oops. "Did you like it?"

He growled, and the hair on her arms stood on end.

He pushed through a door, slamming it shut behind them and engaging the lock. "I want to fuck you," he said.

She didn't think it was a question, or that he was asking for approval. More like a warning as he kept her in his arms and carried her to the farthest corner of the room.

He plopped her down on something cold and hard, his hands slamming on either side of her hips as he leaned in nose to nose with her. "I want to fuck you right *now*."

His hands were on the snap of her bra, pulling it apart

and tossing the fabric aside. He caught the bikini bottoms and stripped them away, the shredded material fluttering to the floor as he ripped opened his pants and set his erection free.

The curtains beside them were open a crack, enough to spotlight the dust motes floating in the air as he pushed her knees open and crushed their bodies together.

His lips were on hers, his hands on her breasts, teasing and tugging at her nipples until she gasped into his mouth.

He bent to lick them, one side then the other. Lillie leaned back on her arms as he worked his way down her body. He caught her ankles and propped them beside her hips a second before he put his mouth to her sex.

Dancing had been all the foreplay she needed, but this? There was no way she could turn this down. He ate hungrily, greedily licking until she squirmed. His tongue targeted her clit, and intense pleasure went off like a flaming arrow, igniting the rest of her body.

Orgasm came rapidly. She burnt to a cinder, nothing but ashes left. He blew, and the embers flared as her body jolted through multiple aftershocks.

She was in the air again, briefly. Flipped to her stomach, her feet dangling toward the floor. Her ass stuck out over the edge of the hard wooden surface. For the first time she got a good look at where she was—sprawled over the satiny smooth finish of a baby grand piano.

"Oh dear. What if someone walks into the room?"

His hands were firm on her hips as he tugged her back, the heated length of his erection rock hard against her butt as he leaned over and put his lips near her ear. "If someone comes in, I hope they plan on playing something lively."

He lined himself up with her pussy and pushed, driving deep as her air rushed out in a gasp. "Oh, *God*."

"Just Jim."

He retreated slowly, so slowly she moaned for a good minute, it seemed. Which was a mistake because that meant when he thrust forward, she had no air left in her lungs and no way to suck any in either.

There was no chance to coordinate her breathing, her lungs starving for oxygen, but she didn't give a damn because he was moving faster. Driving forward, her legs rocking in midair as his groin slapped her ass. The sounds of sex and their heavy breathing echoed in the silence of the room.

And when he came, it was with a roar that shattered the silence and set her blood pumping all over again.

Her heated cheek rested on the cool wood of the piano, her hair tousled everywhere. The sheen of sweat on her skin was beginning to dry, and as he pulled free, she figured she was pretty much a mess.

She didn't care one bit, turning eagerly as he helped her sit up on the piano top. His arms wrapped around her, one hand firm on the back of her neck as he took her lips in a final kiss. Tender this time, gentle.

As if their wildness had been consumed until all that was left was sheer pleasure, joyfully shared between them.

8

Splashing noises escaped from the bathroom along with a saucy tune rendered in a surprisingly fine alto. Jim caught himself tapping his fingers to Lillie's singing, and put aside the newspaper he'd been attempting to read.

It made no sense to be wasting his time in the living room when what he wanted was to spend time with Lillie.

He knocked on the partially open door, and the singing stopped abruptly.

"May I come in?"

More splashing. "Umm, I'm in the bathtub."

The sheer innocence in her voice only made Jim smile harder. "I had surmised that. It's part of the reason I want to come in."

Lillie laughed. "Well, I suppose it is your bathroom."

He'd begun to move as soon as she'd given the first word of approval, strolling to the edge of the tub and looking down on a vision.

There was something about this woman that pleased him so well. Only hours ago they'd shared the most incredible sex at the dance club, and already he wanted her again. And yet, leaning back on the counter, he was content to fold his arms and simply look his fill.

She'd piled her hair on top of her head, and even in the muted feature lighting, coppery highlights glittered as she moved. The claw-toed tub was filled nearly to the brim, her feet nowhere near reaching the end. Her arms were draped over the sides, probably in an attempt to keep herself from sliding under the surface.

No bubbles blocked the view of paradise relaxing before him. Her breasts bobbed along the water's surface, her back slightly arched. A perfect artist's model with one leg bent upward, the other extended. The lean line of her stomach led down to a neat triangle of reddish curls.

Her toenails were painted blue.

He'd seen her naked a number of times already, and every time he enjoyed it more.

Lillie laid her head on the rim of the tub, and her body floated upward. "Did you decide where we're going for dinner?"

"We're staying in." The words burst from him without advance warning. He wasn't sure where the idea had come from, but it was perfect. "If you don't have your heart set on something, we can take it easy. Hang out here, maybe watch a movie."

She blinked her hazel eyes, pulling herself back to vertical and nodding slowly. "Okay. Actually, you know, I would like that very much."

"Good." He sank to his knees beside the tub and went to trickle his fingers through the water, snatching them back as the temperature damn near scalded him. "Lord, woman, how can you stand the water that hot?"

Lillie opened her mouth to answer...and paused. Her

lashes fluttered, and he wondered if she was avoiding sharing something personal.

The lack of information between them clicked over from a logical necessity to an unwanted burden, and suddenly he wanted nothing more than for her to share. He needed to know more about her. Wanted her to know about him.

Warning, warning. There are only two days until the race. Don't do anything foolish.

Jim didn't wait to hear what the other half of his psyche would suggest in response. He wanted...more. Not sure yet what, but they could figure it out as they went along.

His mental ramblings had taken a few seconds, because when he focused, she had turned toward him, all rosy-skinned and smiling. "You're daydreaming," she teased.

"I am, and that's a terrible thing considering I don't need to dream when you're right here in front of me." He caught her fingers in his hand, lifting them to his mouth.

Drops of water fell as he pressed his lips to her knuckles, and Lillie sighed. "I love when you do that. That kiss-the-knuckles thing gets me every time."

Jim gave her fingers a squeeze. "I like it as well."

"You are obviously a well-adjusted and bright individual." She raised a brow. "Are you going to let me out of the tub? Or did you want to join me?"

"Tempting." And it was... "But I think I'll go make dinner arrangements. Any requests? You can have anything you'd like—even the finest restaurants in the area deliver."

She wiggled onto her knees, leaning her hands on the edge of the tub as she pressed her lips to his for a brief, flirtatious kiss. "You're going to think it's silly."

"Try me."

Lillie bestowed another of those delicately sweet kisses

on him before rocking back out of reach. "Pizza? Something with a kick?"

He could do that. "One pizza with a kick, coming right up." He took a final appreciative glance before leaving her, the singing starting up as if the bluebird of happiness had invaded his suite.

She wasn't singing when she joined him, but another of his oversized plain white shirts had found its way from his closet onto her petite form. He didn't mind at all. They looked better on her than they did on him.

Jim held out a hand, and she joined him, curling her fingers around his and curling her body tight as well. "Did you check the movies?" He led her to the couch and seated her, passing over the remote control. "Let me get us something to drink, and you're in charge of this."

Lillie gave an exaggerated gasp of disbelief. "Not the remote control. Really? Really?"

She was almost as bad as Damon. "Did you want to pick the movie tonight or did you want me?"

She cradled the remote to her chest and rocked slightly. "I will cherish it forever."

"You've never even watched TV with me. What makes you think I'm a remote-control hog?"

"You're a guy."

"Women hog the controls as well."

A low clicking noise escaped her. "Statistical data would suggest that in nine out of ten cases of *remote control obnoxia*, the overwhelming majority of sufferers are male."

She tossed him a brilliant smile and turned to the TV, clicking the unit on then tucking the remote into her cleavage.

"If that's where the controls are going to be stored, I can see exactly why men want to have their hands on them."

Too much laughter followed, until Jim's cheeks damn near hurt from all the smiling. She found them a show to watch. The pizza arrived. The next three hours passed in the blink of an eye. Jim couldn't remember having as much fun without sex involved in a long time.

She pointed out plot holes in the movie, just like Jim always got in hell for doing with Damon. At one point, the two of them were so busy discussing what exactly had jumped the shark in the show, they had to rewind to get up to speed with the rest of the action.

He'd ordered three pizzas, pleased to see she had no qualms about eating heartily. Every time she opened the box for herself, she picked up a new slice for him and laid it on his plate. She also went to his fridge and rummaged around until she found something green and leafy. That went on his plate as well, and when he made a face, she tapped her foot and refused to give him any more pizza until he'd eaten his veggies.

She blew bubbles in her soda. Tickled him to make him move and give her more room on the couch.

Jim Halcyon wasn't sure what was happening, but he liked it.

The movie time slipped into talking time, the credits rolling past unobserved as they discussed the cinematography. She was smart and intelligent, and made him think hard when she pointed out inequalities in the casting that he'd completely missed.

They moved in front of the windows, the temperatures having dropped too low to make sitting on the balcony comfortable for Lillie in only his shirt. And no way would he suggest she put on any more clothes.

They could still see the fountain display. She curled up affectionately at his side in the manner he'd grown to crave.

Such an honest sensation, all of her shy trepidation evaporated as he'd earned her trust.

"I think my mom would enjoy the fountain," Lillie shared, "but there's no way my dad would ever come to Vegas."

Something personal.

Very personal, talking about family, and Jim worried he might push too far but he needed to take the chance. "He doesn't like gambling?"

"He doesn't like…" She frowned, this time not as if she was trying to keep secrets, but as if she was trying to figure out the best way to explain. "Dad likes routine, and being at home. And my mom does too, but she's more willing to try new things than him. She was the one who moved to be with him. He's lived his whole life in the same community."

Typical bear situation. His parents had dealt with the same thing, but then discovered they both liked traveling. Liked each other—which didn't always happen.

Jim stroked her fingers where they lay on his thigh. "Are they happy?"

She nodded. "Pretty much. Their life is nothing dazzling or thrilling, but you know—it's not boring, either. It's what they chose, and because of that, yeah, I guess they are happy."

Happiness. Such an elusive thing.

Jim knew how to make his bear happy, and how to make his cock happy. He knew how to complete a business deal in a way that made his bank account happy, but he wasn't sure if he knew how to simply *be happy*. "You know this ride I'm going on with Damon on Friday?"

"Your yearly special thingy? It's not always a ride, is it?"

"Not at all. Every year it's a bet, though. A chance to

win the beautiful coin we purchased together back when we were young."

Her eyes lit up. "That sounds fun. I'm glad you've got something to look forward to." She sat at attention, turning to face him and stroking his shoulders. "Traditions can be really exciting."

Between one heartbeat and the next, all the light faded from her hazel-green eyes, leaving them listless and sad. He was about to demand what the hell had happened when she perked up, her usual enthusiastic self back and demanding he finish his earlier comment.

"What about your ride?"

He trailed his fingers over hers, needing the contact. "The coin isn't worth much, not really. But it's like a lucky talisman, and whoever wins the race gets to keep her for the coming year."

Lillie nodded even as concern flooded her expression. "You know there's not truly anything like a lucky coin, or a magic spell, or anything like that that can swoop in and change your life."

He laughed. "Damon and you could have rehearsed this. Yes, I know luck is hard work and good timing. And it's not that I'm looking for luck, not really."

Or was he?

"Maybe I just need a chance to turn the corner. One moment in time when I say *now things will be different*."

"Is your life so terrible now?" she asked, her hands flying up to cover her mouth briefly. "I'm sorry, that's awfully forward of me. And I'm not trying to snoop, but it seems to me the past few days we've had a good time, and you're a great guy. Why do things need to turn a corner?"

Stroking her skin did more for his nerves than a full-body massage or a gallon of whiskey. It was as if she poured in comfort through osmosis.

"It's been a rough year. I lost my parents last May."

She made a low noise, her hands brushing his briefly. "I'm so sorry. An accident?"

"Cave-in. They were at an archeological site in northern Russia. Not their job—just their passion. An ancient shifter site, so very low profile in terms of development and news. I was there that week visiting."

Too many memories to hold back. He pushed past them and allowed the words to escape.

"Dad had taken me into the cave to show me around when a tremor struck. We could see daylight ahead of us, the opening was that close. He pushed me ahead of him, and in the midst of the chaos I simply ran. I thought he was right on my tail. Only when I glanced back, he'd turned. Headed back to get my mom—I didn't know she was working farther down the dig."

If he couldn't have seen Lillie's face it would have made it easier to keep going. But she was right there, tears gathering in her eyes.

Made it damn hard to stop his heartache from rising.

"Neither of them made it out?" she whispered.

He shook his head. "I got trapped for three days myself. When we finally excavated far enough to find their bodies, they were gone. They had their arms wrapped around each other as if they'd refused to let go, even in death."

She was weeping, tears pouring silently down her cheeks as she crawled right into his lap and offered him comfort.

He sat there, holding her. Thought about all of his accomplishments over the years. The tricks he'd gotten up to, and the mischief and fooling around and...

Some of what he'd spent time on seemed senseless, but like Lillie had pointed out with her parents, he'd chosen to do the things he did. And that made his life right in one way.

Made him empty as well.

"If I ever find the kind of love that my parents had? I wouldn't need Lady Luck. Because they had something more precious, more valuable and far, far more rare than any lucky coin."

9

She woke earlier than him, the same as she had all the other mornings. But this time, instead of crawling away as quietly as she could, she stayed put. Staring at his face and wondering how on earth she could survive.

She'd fallen in love.

That *wasn't* supposed to happen. In all the rules of having a final fling, it was supposed to be about having a good time and lots of sex. Period.

She couldn't even do a simple fling right.

Jim rolled to his side, his arms curling around her possessively. Their limbs were tangled together, one of his big thighs pushed between hers. She wasn't sure if he was trying to stop her from running away, but even the amusement of thinking that faded as she realized this was the last morning she'd be able to consider sneaking out of his bed.

Addie had warned her she was too tender hearted. The fact her friend would be sad at being correct didn't make the situation any better.

Lillie stroked Jim's face, running her fingers through his hair and enjoying the rasp of his morning beard against her palm. She wanted to lean in and kiss him, but then he might wake up and make love to her, like he had last night after he'd shared about his loss.

So tender and caring and...

And if he did it again, she really didn't think she could stop herself from blurting out her terrible secret.

She was the biggest fool in Vegas, and that was saying something.

It was no use. She eased from underneath him. Jim complained softly, but didn't wake.

Lillie tugged on his shirt because she couldn't bear not having his scent around her. She wondered if she swiped the garment, how long it would continue to smell like him after she was gone.

She opened her computer, heading straight to her email. Her IM pinged immediately with a message from Addie. Lillie stared at it, debating if her friend had a tracking device that let her know exactly when to administer a swift kick.

How are you doing, bb?

Was there even an answer to that? *You're right, I'm not cut out to have a fling*

There was silence for a moment as her bestie figured out what she was talking about.

Oh, sweetie. I'm so sorry

It's okay. I'll be okay

Do you want me to do anything? Do you need me to call anyone, or get on a plane and kick some butt? Because I'm there for you. I really really am. You deserve to be happy, bb

And right then and there, Lillie's heart skipped. She popped up from her computer and paced the room.

Holy cow. Addie was right.

She *did* deserve to be happy. There was no reason why she shouldn't simply figure out a way to take all the happiness she'd experienced this past week and make it a forever thing.

It wasn't as if she were heading off to meet the love of her life. Ritual and routine be damned. If she hadn't found Jim, then she would've been fine going along with tradition.

But she *had* found Jim.

Only...she had no confirmation he felt the same way about her. Was she going to throw away her future and potentially piss off some important bigwigs, and her parents, on the off-chance the big grizzly wanted her for more than just a fling?

No question. Damn *right* she was going to take a shot at it.

She raced back to the computer and signed off so rapidly she was sure Addie would send text messages every five minutes until she responded.

And Lillie would tell her more, once she made it safely onto a plane.

Because while she didn't know for sure that Jim wanted her, she now knew what it was like to fall in love, and she wasn't going to give that up for anything in the world.

If it turned out after all was said and done, Jim simply wanted a fling? She'd pull up her big-girl panties and accept...

Little mental sirens went off instantly. *Awoooo, awoooo, bullshit warning.*

Nope, she wasn't going to accept anything *except* Jim falling one hundred percent and completely head-over-heels in love with her. No matter how long it took, and *that* was the truth.

But in the meantime, she had a contract to dissolve. She'd reached a fork in the road, and it was time *she* chose the path she followed.

She made a quick call to the front desk to order a taxi. Then she went to work, hacking into the plane registry she'd accessed five days ago. Because she needed transportation, stat, to get where she was going. Even if her methods were a touch on the illegal side.

Five minutes later, she slipped on her shoes and coat, grabbing the small bag Jim had bought her. She had her finger hovering over the call button for the elevator when she realized there was one more task to complete. She darted back into the room to grab a notepad.

Nothing. How could a grown man who claimed to be a workaholic have absolutely nothing in the place to use to leave a note?

Desperate, she grabbed the empty pizza boxes from their dinner, flipped one over and used coloured lip balm to write a message.

Something I need to do. Gone for 2 days at least. I know your race starts tomorrow. Have fun with Damon. Contact you when I can.

There was so much more she wanted to say, but she was out of lip balm and out of time. She dropped her message on the coffee table and fled the apartment before he woke up and stopped her.

Because her vanishing for a short while was the only solution.

~

She was gone.

Jim curled upright, wondering how in the hell she

managed it every morning, but this time round his puzzlement was tinged with amusement instead of frustration.

He hadn't woken in a cold sweat from being alone in bed. It was as if her presence had remained with him, helping him know someone cared.

It was time to move on.

Damon had expressed his concerns about Lillie, but the biggest thing he'd been right about was the secrecy. It was time for their secret-keeping to be over. Jim was going to find out everything there was to know about Lillie, because he intended to have her around for a long, long time.

He strolled into the living area.

She wasn't at the coffee table working on her computer.

She wasn't in the kitchen making coffee.

He double-checked the bathroom, and the guest room, but she hadn't been hiding in there either.

What the hell?

Then he spotted the pizza box, disbelief rising as he read her message with growing concern.

Dammit, he needed his phone now, no more farting around.

He stomped to the landline and pushed a couple buttons. "Get me the phone I ordered, and find Damon Black. Tell him I need his ass up here right now."

What the hell did *something I need to do* mean? Forget about looking for a needle in a haystack, he truly had no idea where she was headed. He forced himself to get dressed so he would be ready to run on a moment's notice.

Damon and the phone arrived at the same time.

"What happened? You look as if someone died."

"She's gone." Jim dragged a hand through his hair. "I woke up alone and she's gone and she said there's something she needs to do, and I'm supposed to go on the damn ride with you, but fuck that, I need to find out where she is."

"Lillie's gone?" Damon glanced toward the corner of the room, his face folding into a frown. "But all of her luggage is still here."

For the first moment since Jim had discovered her missing, he actually got a full breath of air. Okay, maybe she *was* planning on coming back. "But where is she? What if she's in trouble and needs my help?"

"Or what if..." Damon wrinkled his nose. "Look. I know I read you the riot act yesterday, but you were right. I had no proof anything was wrong. So what if she simply went to tell Mommy and Daddy she's planning on staying in Vegas for a while? Did you think of that?"

Jim was far too worried for logic. "She could have said that."

"Well, she did say she'd get in touch with you in a few days. She's been pretty honest until now, so maybe you should take her word for it." Damon clapped his hands. "Tell you what. We'll head out tomorrow, and by the time we come back—"

"I need to know where she is, now," Jim roared.

He hauled his new phone from the envelope Damon had passed him and waited for it to boot up.

Damon squeezed his shoulder. "Okay, bro, since you've got your panties in a twist, I'll do what I can to help you. Hey, how did you end up with a phone already?"

"I ordered it right after you destroyed mine, dumbass."

A million emails downloaded onto the remote access, his voice box filling to the brim. Jim tried to remember if he'd ever gotten Lillie's phone number. He pressed play and held the phone to his ear as he shouted orders at Damon. "Check with the front desk and see if anybody saw her leave. That will at least give us something to go on. Then check—"

The message in his ear distracted him from his immediate task. He came to a complete stop for a full minute before the cursing welled up and burst free. "Shit. *Shit.* Fuckdamnfuckers *shit.*"

Damon frowned. "What?"

"Listen."

Jim hit play, watching his astounded friend's expression turn to dismay as the recording continued.

"Mr. Halcyon. We are pleased to inform you that we at the Ursus Planning Board have been working diligently to find you a suitable partner. As you know, your name was added to our list when you reached the age of majority, but with our fierce attention to maintaining a stellar track record, it's taken until now to find a proper mate for your particular needs.

"Just this last week we were contacted by the family of a lovely young lady who we believe will be a wonderful addition to your clan. She has concluded her education, and in finalization of our contract, she is en route to join you.

"We trust this arrangement will meet with your satisfaction, and that your marriage will proceed as expected within the next short timeframe. If you have any questions or concerns, please contact the main UPB office during regular office hours. We thank you for your business. Have a nice day."

Damon and Jim exchanged horrified glances.

"You're not serious. You signed up for a mail-order bride? How come I never knew this?" Damon demanded.

"Because of course you knew. It's the way we bears always do things. We don't have fated mates like you wolves, and if it was left up to us, all bear shifters would be gone within two generations. So they set up the Board to arrange marriages." Jim clenched his fist and growled at the ceiling. "I do not need this right now," he shouted at the heavens.

"I can't believe this is something you need at any time," Damon boggled. "You have a woman en route to your home who expects to marry you... Are you expected to just drop everything and go?"

He looked totally confused, and disgusted, and dismayed all at the same time.

Jim was grabbing his coat and his passport. "Normally, yes. That's exactly what is expected."

"That's crazy."

"That's how most bear shifters do it," Jim spoke slowly and steadily, fighting the rising anger in his gut. "I don't want this, okay? Yes, even a week ago I would've been fine with it, but there is no way I want to drop everything I've got right now to go play happy families with some stranger."

He slipped on his shoes.

"Where are you going?" Damon asked. "You're not still thinking you can find Lillie, are you?" His eyes widened. "Oh shit. What're you going to do about her?"

"One thing at a time. It's not this woman's fault she's been chosen to be my bride. I can't just send her a phone message and tell her to go home. It's possible I'm going to have to do some fast-talking to get out of this contract, but I *have* to get out of it. Plus, I need to find Lillie, but I can only do one thing at a time. And that means I have to go to Whitehorse first."

"Or you could forget all of them, say screw the whole business and we take off for an extended bike trip." Damon raised a brow. "There's still Lady Luck on the line. I handed her in to the judge yesterday, and the man is not going to give her back to anyone who hasn't met the requirements we arranged."

Jim stilled for all of half a second. "Screw Lady Luck."

"Seriously?" His friend's jaw hung open. "You know damn well you have a better chance in this race than I do. Your bike is faster and you're a better rider than I am. You're really willing to throw away your chance to win rather than staying here for one more day, two tops, and getting it done? I mean, the woman up at your house can sit there for weeks, for all that it matters."

"And what am I going to do when Lillie returns? Tell her I have to go talk to the woman who is supposed to be my wife, so I can break it off with her, but hey, stick around. I should be back in no time." The entire situation had turned crazy so quickly, Jim's head was spinning. "No. You do the ride, and get Lady Luck. I'm going to make my own luck and get what I want. And *who* I want, and it isn't this strange woman, it's Lillie."

"But—"

"Give it up, Damon. It's just a damn coin. Lillie is real flesh and blood and passion, and I'll be damned if I let anything come between us."

Damon stared for a long while before he shook his head. "Okay. I got your back. You track down your betrothed, convince her to return to the old country, and in the meantime, I'll do my best to find your missing lady."

Jim clutched his hands. "Thank you."

"No guarantees that I won't have convinced her I'm the better catch," Damon teased. He ducked Jim's halfhearted swing. "Go on. Fix your fucked-up personal life, and call me if you need anything. I'll keep you up to date."

10

*I*t should have taken him five hours max to go from his condo to McCarran Airport to Whitehorse. Instead, it took twice that long as he scrambled to find transportation. He had to hire a new private plane.

He'd forgotten that part of arranged marriages. When the Board had failed to reach him, they'd probably contacted his assistant who would have ordered the Halcyon plane to pick his fiancée up.

But after a bunch of finagling and crossing palms with cash, Jim finally made it. The snow-lined runway reflected the blinking red and white plane lights as the small jet rolled up to the single-story square building that was the main terminal. He took deep breaths of the icy-cold winter air as he transferred to the ground, marching straight through the building and back out to crawl into the private car waiting for him.

Whitehorse in February. This was why he owned a place in Vegas.

Thirty more minutes to kill as the car headed up the Alaskan Highway from the tiny Whitehorse airport to his home in the mountains. Jim fought to keep from drumming his fingers on the fine leather upholstery.

In his earlier scramble, he'd convinced someone to come up with a name. Katherine Lileas Ruadh. He'd never heard of her, or her clan, giving him even more reason to believe she was a European import. But at least he had that much—the name of the unfortunate woman he was about to send packing.

He stared out the window as the trees grew thicker and the car wove its way up the long approach to his driveway. The sun had already set, but there were twinkling lights visible at moments through the trees.

The last time he'd been in Whitehorse he'd rented a Jeep, hauling his parents along to show them the spot he'd selected for his home.

The aching sensation in his chest wasn't just from missing them. They were gone, and that was always going to hurt, but they'd given him so much and always been there for him when he needed them.

They'd shown him a perfect example of a couple in love.

He wanted that, and he wanted it with Lillie. The sooner he dealt with this escalating situation, the better.

It would be dealt with, though. This wasn't going to ruin him, or his future. He had to reach out and take what he wanted, with both hands, and that he could damn well do.

They approached the front entrance to his home, and curiosity finally won. Updates had arrived on a regular basis from his general contractor, along with the occasional swatch of granite or paint sample to make decisions about. But mostly, after his parents had died, he'd allowed others to deal with the day-to-day issues.

Now he looked up at the home he'd designed, with its grand front entrance, and felt a touch of pride. The wide stairs rose toward massive twin front doors, enormous pillars strategically placed along the entire house frontage that turned the three-story building into a castle in the wilderness.

It was gorgeous, and he let himself out, staring up at his home.

He'd told Damon the truth. A week ago if he'd gotten word his bride was waiting for him, this meeting would have had an entirely different feel to it. Now the excitement of looking around his home was muted by the irritation of having to send away someone who didn't expect his rejection.

This wasn't going to be fun for either of them. He might know what he wanted, but he didn't have to be an asshole about it. He had a fine line to walk, and he really hoped the woman would be reasonable in return.

He brought the heavy brass knocker on the front door down sharply against the doorplate. The ringing sound echoed off the tall walls, and the front door swung open.

The well-dressed young man's smile faded rapidly as he snapped to attention, his gaze skipping over Jim's face. In the process, the huge door in his hands got away from him, and he had to chase after it to stop the heavy weight from slamming into the wall. He brought his flustered self back to attention, body stiff and chin held high as he refused to meet Jim's eyes. "Mr. Halcyon. Please, come in, we've been expecting you."

Jim pressed past him into the foyer, torn between examining every detail of his new home and just getting to the bottom of why he was there. "Where is she?" he demanded.

To his surprise, the doorman stepped back, hands dropping in front of him as he tangled his fingers nervously. "About that, sir. About the lady who arrived earlier today..."

"Yes. My betrothed. Where is she?" Jim asked again, frowning at the delay. Why had the woman not gotten to Whitehorse until today? He'd gotten the message a few days ago.

"It's just that... I mean, I want to prepare you, sir. She seems a trifle more nervous than most brides-to-be. She's been acting strangely ever since she got here, and I thought..." The youth swallowed hard. "You're rather intimidating to meet for the first time, sir."

Good grief. As aware as Jim was of needing to be gentle with the woman, he did not want to waste time coddling his staff. Not when he had things to do.

Still, these were the people who had been hired to help take care of him, even though this boy looked as if he should still be in the nursery. They needed to know he could be trusted.

The fact he could hear Lillie taunting him to be nice kicked his butt, hard. He was itching to take off, but for her sake, he slowed and took the extra time. "What's your name?"

"Peter. Sir." The boy blinked hard, his dark gaze darting away as he fidgeted with the sleeves of his suit coat, but refused to run like he obviously wanted. Bobcat shifter, if Jim scented correctly.

Jim hid his smile. Nothing wrong with the kid's spunk. "Thank you for being honest, and for the warning, and I promise I will tread softly, but you need to tell me where she is."

Peter swung his arm and pointed up the curved

staircase. "I tried taking her to the master suite, but she insisted on being shown to a guest room."

Curious.

"Really." Jim glanced around. He should have known this answer, but he'd been too busy ignoring his northern holdings until ten hours ago. "How many staff on the premises? Just you and a cook? Or more?"

"Full staff, sir, ever since the building was completed a month ago. There are six of us." He flushed. "My mom is your chef. Dad's in charge of cleaning and maintenance."

Ahh, now his baby butler's presence made more sense.

Another thought hit. Great—his staff had been hanging out for a month, everything running nice and quiet, and today would be their first glimpse of their new master in action.

He hoped the girl didn't cry. That would just cement his reputation as a heartless monster. "You gave her the room at the top of the stairs to the right, correct?"

"Yes. Second suite. I can show you."

"I think I'll be fine, Peter. I designed the house."

Jim took the stairs two at a time, grabbing the heavy walnut post at the top and swinging himself onto the landing.

"Be calm and go slow. Be calm, and go slow," he muttered.

Stupid. He needed one of those signs that said: *Be calm and have a double shot of whiskey.*

A colourful piece of paper caught his eye. It had been folded into an elaborate three-dimensional origami star, and it looked totally out of place on the delicate antique table that had obviously been moved from its regular position along the wall to a spot in the middle of the hall. The note had his name written on some of the outstretched prongs, and he picked up the creation with a rising sense of dismay.

He didn't want her writing love notes, and that's what the bright pink paper seemed to indicate.

But the actual contents of the page surprised him. When he unfolded the sheet of construction paper all he discovered was his name on the front, and on the opposite side the words *We need to talk.*

He walked slower, his shoes sinking into the thick, plush carpet, the massive windows facing to the south, dark and cold. Only the table lamps and wall sconces cast golden glows on the pristine wallpaper and plaster, warming his path.

Another piece of paper, this one folded into a bright green tree, sat on the floor, and he stooped to grab it. Inside, her writing went from neat to messy, as if she'd written in a hurry or she'd grown more agitated in the process.

I'm sorry for leading you on.

Jim blinked. That made no sense at all. Just who was this woman he'd been sent?

Next note: a pale blue bird shape, the dark black writing bold and firm in contrast, and this time Jim swore, not believing his eyes as the message appeared. *I was fine with marrying you up until a week ago, but now I can't.*

Holy. Shit.

Maybe this was going to work out better than he thought. He followed the trail of notes down the hall, snatching them up and reading with a rapidly rising hope.

Red, folded into the shape of a maple leaf: *I've fallen in love with a wonderful man—well, I think he's wonderful. I haven't told him that yet.*

Two more steps to reach an orange circle, like a shining sun: *He deserves love, and so do I.*

A purple crescent moon hung balanced on the edge of a lamp beside the guest room: *So, I hope you'll be okay with us breaking our engagement.*

Yellow, the paper simply folded and tucked into the doorframe: *Um, I'm a little scared to tell you this in person, but I knew I had to be brave enough to say it.*

Jim knocked on the door. "Katharine? May I come in?"

No answer.

He tried twice more before abandoning his manners and cracking the door open.

No one was there. God, he hoped she hadn't done something stupid like jump out the window. Strangely, there was no sign of any bags, or anything of hers.

Another note waited for him on the pristine bed. A plain white piece of paper.

He picked this one up and crossed his fingers for no final surprises.

If you're done being growly, I'm waiting in the kitchen.

He considered dancing a jig, right there and then. The whole mess could be straightened out in a few minutes. He'd pop his ex-fiancée on a plane, rushing her home to her sweetheart with his blessing, then be back on the hunt for Lillie before he'd had a coffee.

On second thought, he might stay for an hour or two— look around the house and meet the staff. Let them know he intended to return soon with his *real* partner.

You could make it back to Vegas in time to join Damon. You could still do the road race, his ambition enticed.

Fat fucking chance of that.

Lady Luck means nothing to me. Shut up, and let me concentrate.

He didn't need the coin anymore—he needed his

copper-headed goddess with the willing laugh and bright smile who'd beguiled his heart.

Jim tucked the final note with the others in his hand, and headed to the kitchen to tell his fiancée goodbye.

∽

She'd been sitting on pins and needles for the last eight hours, and she was tired and worried. The day had been one nightmare on her nerves after another. First she'd had to screw up her courage to face the airport, sweet-talk her way past the private-plane attendants, and then stew for the entire four-hour flight from Vegas to Whitehorse as she practiced turning down her future husband.

And *then* the bastard didn't have the decency to be home when she got there. Instead, she'd gotten extra time to fuss and worry herself into a tizzy. Only the memory of Jim's touch and the look of tenderness in his eyes gave her the courage to keep going forward.

The house she'd been brought to was incredible, but Lillie couldn't feel sad at turning down marriage to the man who owned such a fabulous retreat. She could have happily lived there—more comfortable than in busy Vegas—but it was the man she wanted, not the setting.

Whoever had said location, location, location hadn't been talking about the heart.

All the staff at the mansion were wonderful as well. They went out of their way to ease her fears, though at the same time some of what they shared made things scarier.

They had never even seen the man she was supposed to marry—he'd refused to come to any events in the area. He'd given lists of what he expected to have available at all times, but never shown up to see his will was obeyed.

He didn't need to worry on that account. No one dared to take a chance the head of the Halcyon clan was one of the tyrant types who were whispered about in the bear community.

Lillie had the file Addie had sent her filled with all sorts of juicy gossip about the man. She'd refused to look at it. It was bad enough she was there to tell him goodbye. Nope. Details about Jamieson Halcyon could stay a mystery.

Lillie shot to her feet as the sweet young doorman who'd been so nice to her slipped through the doors.

"He's gone upstairs." Peter patted her shoulder kindly. "He looked a lot less fierce than I expected. Why don't you stay here? We'll make sure everything is fine."

She closed her eyes and wrapped her arms around herself in a hug. Summoning the courage she'd need in the next few moments.

Around her the smells of cooking helped center her, something simmering on the stove. A soothing rattle of pots and pans washed over her as Peter's mom and another woman worked together, their voices low as they conversed.

Peter didn't say anything more, but stood nearby and looked protective.

And then Jim walked in.

Lillie's stomach fell all the way to her toes.

"Oh no. *No.*" Too many things slammed through her brain as she took in the shock of him being in exactly the wrong place. How had he...? Why...?

This was *not* good.

"What are you doing here?" She rushed forward, fisting her hands in his jacket and going up on her tiptoes to try to get in his face. "I told you I would be coming back. You can't be here, not now. It's not safe."

The last thing she needed was the man she loved getting into a fight with the man she was supposed to marry.

A crease formed between Jim's brows. "What do you mean, it's not safe?"

She gave up on tugging him, instead pushing hard and attempting to shove him back toward the door. Maybe if she got him outside she could convince him to hide until she'd spoken with her betrothed.

"I have to talk to someone, and he's not going to be happy with me. And I don't want you here and getting in a fight, so please, go away."

She should have known pushing him would be as successful as trying to move the Great Wall of China.

"Lillie. Stop trying to tip me over, and let's see if you can make sense."

"I don't know how you managed to track me down," she protested. "But I'm sure if you give me a while I can convince my fiancé to call it off—"

"Fiancé?"

Lillie squeezed her eyes together, slapping her hands over her ears. She didn't want to hear or see what came next.

Strong fingers wrapped around her wrists and gently tugged her hands loose. Jim moved close enough heat passed between their bodies. He let go of one hand and pressed his fingers under her chin, tilting her face upward.

Only he didn't say anything. He kept staring into her eyes, while he barked out an order at the staff. "All of you. Get out, now."

"But, sir—"

"Out." The word was said quietly, but with a force of nature behind the command.

Lillie wasn't surprised to discover the staff had

abandoned her. No matter how brave they were, she wouldn't have disobeyed that tone of voice, either.

But this was Jim. *Her Jim*, and she knew he'd never do anything to harm her. She sighed heavily and tried to reason with the big beast. "Promise me you won't get into a fight with him."

His lips twitched. "With your fiancé, you mean?"

She dipped her chin as much as his fingers would allow.

Jim held a hand in the air, his expression going completely solemn. "I swear to not lay a hand on the man."

Lillie let out the breath she'd been holding. "I still have no idea how you found me, but if you'll just let me—"

He didn't let her say another word. Instead, he kissed her, holding their lips in sensual contact while his right hand slipped to her back so he could crush their torsos together. Lillie gave up trying to push him away, instead clinging tight. Giving him back her caresses. After less than a day apart, she craved his touch.

She was dizzy by the time he let her come up for air.

Jim pressed his fingers over her lips when she would have protested. "I want to know every single detail I missed asking you about earlier, but first, let me make sure of something. Is your name Katherine Lileas Ruadh?"

Oh. My. Word.

The only way he would know that would be... And that would mean...

"Halcyon? You're the head of the Halcyon clan?" She gave herself a mental kick. How stupid had it been for her *not* to read the information Addie had dug up on him?

Jim picked her up and sat her on the island counter, his arms resting on either side of her hips as he moved in close, smile growing broader. "Well, of all the mistakes I've made over the years, you are one of the best."

"*You're* my fiancé?"

"I am, and you're mine, Lillie. Mine forever, and I'm keeping you." He paused, pulling the notes she'd painstakingly written from his pocket. He shook the mass of them in the air. "Oh, and this other bastard you're in love with? Fuck him. He's not here to protect his own, so he's out of the picture."

The shock of discovering she'd been fooling around with the man she'd been sent to marry was reduced by amusement that he was already making jokes about it. Lillie cupped his face. "Silly boy."

Jim leaned forward, his expression heating up. "Not a boy, but a full-grown bear. You ready for me?"

"Do I have a choice?" Lillie teased.

"No." He shook his head, gaze boldly undressing her before his hands followed through, slowly stripping her as he continued to grill her. "I do have one final question—or two. How did you get to Vegas? That phone message I got from the Board was sent a week ago. You should have been flown straight from Glasgow to Whitehorse."

Her cheeks brightened. "I'm a hack."

He didn't get it, the blinking confusion in his dark brown eyes all too clear.

She sighed. "I like to play with computers, and cracking people's security systems is a hobby. I don't do anything bad once I'm in—it's just for the challenge—but that's why my family informed the Board I was ready for marriage. They were tired of keeping an eye on me, and I 'disrupt the peaceful serenity of the household'."

"Oh, lovely," he said, amusement clearly rising. "I hope they don't expect *me* to keep you under control?"

"I think that was their plan, but you're far too nice to stop me from having fun, right?"

She batted her lashes, and Jim burst out laughing. "You are trouble. Finish your story. How did you get to Vegas?"

"When I discovered the plane was coming to get me, I broke into your system, and found out which airports it had been to in the past while. I figured a change of flight to a recent destination wouldn't raise any suspicions."

He nodded, gliding his thumbs along her collar bone. "Tricky. I used the plane to get to Vegas the day before you arrived."

"I felt terrible when I heard your staff had done back-to-back Transatlantic crossings." She shivered as his exploration trailed down over the top of her nipples, circling once, then heading south. "I think you need to give them bonuses."

All his attention was on his right hand as he pressed his palm to her belly, fingertips now aimed downward. "You don't have an accent..."

The question was there, unasked.

"Aye, an accent 'tis a fine thing, to be true, but there be no reason to talk like a Scots when you been up to finishing school in both London and New York." Lillie warmed inside as his face lit up at her deliberately thick brogue.

"You need to talk dirty to me sometime with the accent," Jim suggested, brushing his cheek against her shoulder. The scruff on his chin teasing her senses. "I want to hear you say 'put your cock in mah poussy and fock me harrrrrd' with that lovely lilt."

She covered her mouth, hiding her gasp as he opened her folds with his fingertips. "Perchance, I may oblige."

One stroke after another followed until he had her squirming. He slipped two fingers into her core, his thumb magically finding her clit and pushing it like an emergency stop button.

It was too late. Sirens were already going off in her head.

"But right now," Jim murmured, "it's not the dirty words I want. I want to hear you say the other words. You wrote them down, but I want to know you meant them for me."

Lillie pressed her hands to his arms, the fine linen of his suit jacket smooth and warm under her hands. His thick biceps bulging the fabric.

He looked into her eyes. "I love you, Lillie. Maybe this is too fast, and yet I've been waiting for you my entire life. I love you, and want you to move in with me, wherever we choose. I want you to be my wife. My lover. My friend."

The entire time he spoke, his fingers didn't stop moving. Lillie clung to his arms, needing an anchor to keep her from floating off the countertop.

"Everything else we'll figure out later, but this part we've already got. And it doesn't matter how many times I say it, I'm never going to get tired of how it sounds." He stopped, his fingers deep inside her. As if he couldn't leave her—as if he *needed* to have her with him.

She didn't want to wait, but she wasn't going to give him what he wanted until she got what she wanted as well. Lillie scrambled for his zipper and pulled his cock free, wiggling her hips to the edge of the counter.

Jim was just as eager, grasping the root of his thick shaft to line them up perfectly. Then they both watched as he slid into her all the way. Deeper than his fingers, deep enough she trembled.

So deep they were one person, and she never wanted them to be apart.

"I love you," she whispered.

Jim pulled back just so he could press forward all over.

He repeated the move three times, a half dozen, until she lost track. Until they were both gasping. His speed increased, rubbing her clit perfectly as he arched over her and ground his pelvis against her on every stroke.

And his eyes—mesmerizing. A magnet holding her gaze. He teased his thumb over her clit, and her climax hit.

That's when he said it again.

"I love you."

Locked together, arms wrapped around each other's torsos, touching intimately. Their hearts as one.

It could have been hours later when they finally loosened from their clinch. His breath made her hair sway as he clutched her, his forehead pressed to her neck. Then a low chuckle shook his chest, growing louder and harder as she ran her hands over his shoulders.

Jim spoke, the words rumbling out lusty and full of happiness. "I'm sorry for ruining your bucket list."

Lillie lifted her fingers to straighten his hair, sensual satisfaction still pounding through her veins as she pondered the comment. "When did you ruin my bucket list?"

He grinned as he pulled out and tucked things away. "You wanted to have a final fling before going to meet your fiancé. You failed."

Oops. "I didn't do that very well, did I?" Mischievous thoughts danced in her brain, and she didn't attempt to rein them in. "Well, we're not married yet. So, you know, if we go back to Vegas, I bet I could convince Damon—"

Jim's growl was back, echoing through the kitchen loud enough to set the pots hanging over the stove swaying. Lillie wiggled off the counter, darting out of reach and flipping through the doorway back to the foyer.

He chased her, his mocking roars mixing with her laughter as she dashed up the stairs and headed for safety.

"You'd better be headed to our bedroom, wench," he warned.

She paused at the top of the stairs, eyeing all the doors lining the wall, and wondered which one hid the master suite. "Shit, you build them big."

Strong arms caught her up, and he smiled happily as he carried her to the proper room. "I'm a grizzly. We do everything bigger."

EPILOGUE

*J*im strolled the hallway, his fingers tangled in Lillie's. She continued to chatter on about something she'd discovered during her trip into Whitehorse, and it wasn't that he was ignoring her...

He was so delighted with how well things had turned out over the past couple weeks, he couldn't focus on her words because he was completely obsessed with the woman uttering them.

He tugged her to a stop, settling onto the bench overlooking the grand foyer and lifting her into his lap so he could stare at her face. "Tell me again."

"I was in town this morning, and the Alpine Bakery is even more delicious than Peter told me." She traced her hands along his collar, straightening him with the easy affection he'd come to crave from her. "The local wolf pack are a funny lot. I spotted a bunch of them on Main Street, and they were setting up some kind of dog-sled races. I mean, not in their wolf forms, but in human. It was sweet."

Jim smiled at her enthusiasm. "There's a community

event planned for the weekend. I'll be sure to take you, if only to keep all those wolves from getting to make passes."

"They aren't nearly as stiff and uptight as the wolves in Glasgow."

"Good to know. Not that we need to have much to do with them."

"Well, one of them owns this great computer shop, and she's working on getting better internet service established, so that would be nice." She stuttered to a stop, blushing slightly.

Jim narrowed his gaze. "I thought you gave up hacking."

"I did," she exclaimed, slipping her gaze away as she played with his tie. "Mostly."

"Lillie..."

Her hazel eyes sparkled, amusement rising as she smiled innocently. "Just remember, if you ever need the lowdown on any of your competitors, I'm only a squeeze away."

A loud banging sounded from the front door, drawing their attention. Peter hurried across the pristine granite, pulling the grand doors open as Jim took to his feet, keeping protective watch over Lillie.

He didn't need to worry.

"Jeez, I thought I'd freeze my furry paws off before I ever saw civilization again." Damon untangled a six-foot, bright blue scarf from around his neck and dumped it into Peter's hands, followed by his hat, gloves and oversized winter parka. He glanced at Jim who was guiding Lillie down the stairs. "Why the hell did you build a place so far north? Are you taking over for Santa or some shit? The entire ride up here I kept expecting to see brightly dressed gnomes leaping from tree to tree singing Christmas carols."

"Sorry, you missed them. We sent them off on vacation for a month."

Damon stepped forward, then paused, eyeing his shoes and the wide granite floor.

Jim shook his head. "You're never going to grow up, are you?"

His friend waggled his brows. "Whatever for?"

He took a running start before skidding rapidly toward them, perfectly balanced with his arms extended. Lillie laughed before ducking out of the way.

Damon spun past, completely out of control as he crashed into a side table.

Lillie let go of Jim's arm and hurried over to help the wolf to his feet. "Are you okay?"

"He's fine," Jim growled, folding his arms over his chest and glaring at his friend. "Don't bother being sympathetic. He just wants you to pet him."

"Sir, I am shocked at the accusation." Damon grinned though, slipping his arm around Lillie as he brought her back to Jim's side. "I didn't even try to sneak a kiss."

"That's because you know you'd look funny without your teeth," Lillie commented sweetly, patting his cheek as she escaped his clutches. "And you don't really want poor Jim here to hurt his hand on your face, do you?"

"Of course not." Damon stepped back to a safe distance before lifting his laughing gaze to meet Jim's. "I see you decided against sending the trollop packing."

Jim pinched the bridge of his nose. "Did you have a particular reason you're here? Or did you travel all this way just to annoy me?"

Damon paused. "Actually, I'm a master of multitasking. I thought I could do both..."

Only Lillie's sparkling laughter gave Jim the patience to refrain from threatening Damon with fleas. She caught them both by the hand and backed toward the kitchen. "Come on. I know Mrs. Natty was making cookies this morning."

She danced away, and Jim couldn't stop a sigh of happiness from bursting free.

"You're positively giddy," Damon observed. "Henpecked looks good on you."

"Shut up." He pounded his friend on the back as they cut through the swinging doors into the kitchen. "Some day you'll meet your mate, and I will gloat and taunt and throw you a big party."

Damon slipped to the tall windows overlooking the now snow-filled swimming pool, staring out at the wintery scene. "Sure. If you insist."

In the background, Lillie was discussing a snack with the chef, and Jim watched for a moment as his lovely woman spoke, her hands flying in excitement as she organized, of all things, milk and cookies.

Jim turned away to stand beside his silent friend. "Deep thoughts?"

"Mysteries of the universe. The answer is forty-two. We already know this."

"Ahh, but what's the question?" Jim leaned on the wall beside the window. "Enough blathering. It's good to see you, but I didn't expect you to visit until the spring. You're allergic to snow."

Damon wrinkled his nose in disgust as he stared outside. "Nasty, sticky stuff. Makes great base if you scoop it into a glass and pour liquor over it like civilized people do."

Jim waited. His friend would get to the point eventually. Maybe.

"Come sit by the fire," Lillie commanded them, and Damon and Jim exchanged glances before trotting after her obediently.

The wolf settled into the chair closest to the heat with a long rumble of satisfaction. "This? Makes the trip worthwhile."

"Good to know my fireplace ranks higher than I do," Jim poked.

"Fireplace and *cookies*. Jeez, you'd think I'd pick only the fireplace over you? Some best friend you are."

Lillie snuggled into the loveseat beside Jim and slipped her hands around his arm. "Are you going to stay for a few days?" she asked.

Damon shook his head. "Can't. Got things to do, and I don't feel like checking in with the Takhini pack to let them know I'm around. Too much politics. I can safely stay the night without ruffling too many feathers."

It was a valid point. Wolves were testy about certain things, and Damon was not only a powerful wolf, he had his hot buttons. It wasn't worth getting the local Alpha riled up for a short visit. Jim nodded at the logic, even though... "This summer you can come for longer. We'll know who to talk to by then—you might be able to do your meet-and-greet over the phone or something."

"Maybe." Damon finished munching down his first cookie, his bright eyes matching his blue button-down shirt. He rubbed the crumbs from his fingers and smacked his lips. "Tasty. Anyway, the reason I'm here."

He dug into his pocket and pulled out a small object, extending his hand forward. In his palm a small round disk flashed in the firelight.

"Lady Luck." Jim stared at the artifact. He'd honestly not thought about it once over the past two weeks since chasing after his supposed-wife-slash-turned-out-to-be-Lillie incident.

"Yep." Damon pulled his hand back and stared down at the shiny. "Thought you'd like to know she's safe, and all. Finally convinced the judge to hand her over."

"Good for you."

And he meant it, even when Damon began flipping her into the air, her shimmering copper surface sending streaks of light over the walls as she spun.

"Actually, here's the thing. I knew you were okay with me winning her. You picked Lillie and doing the right thing over this bauble, and I was impressed. So..."

Damon stopped flipping her vertically and instead tossed the coin at Jim.

Only instinct made him move fast enough to catch it, his heart skipping a beat. "What the hell are you doing?"

His friend leaned back in his chair, easing toward the fire's heat. "It's mine to do with what I want for the year, and I want to give it to you. Take it, it's yours."

The skipped beat was back, with friends, as Jim's heart thumped into double-time. He glanced at the copper disk nestled in the palm of his hand, the designs like familiar dreams rushing into his brain. This was what he'd longed for. What had been missing in his life...

He glanced beside him and caught sight of Lillie, a small half-smile teasing her lips. The firelight licked over her hair. She'd taken to wearing it down over her shoulders because he'd asked her to.

Her eagerness to learn more about him delighted him. They'd talked damn near nonstop for the past two weeks. They were only beginning to see how much they belonged together.

She was his love *and* his luck. He tossed the coin back to Damon without another glance. "Keep the trinket. I've got the only lady I need right here."

"Ick. Mushy stuff." In the background Damon mock-sighed in disgust, but it was the brilliant light in Lillie's eyes that held Jim trapped.

"Are you sure?" she asked.

"Positive." He leaned forward, intending to kiss her no matter what noises Damon made. He didn't think she could look any more beautiful, but somehow, it happened.

The entire room lit up as she shot out of his arms and twirled in the middle of the room, her arms stretched to the side as a loud squeal of excitement escaped. Her hair shimmered in the light like fireworks set off in their house. Jim watched in amusement and adoration.

And confusion when she stopped in mid-twirl and thrust out a hand toward Damon. "Mine," she shouted.

"You cheated," his friend grumbled, but he flicked the coin into the air. "I don't know how, but you cheated."

"Did not." She stuck out her tongue briefly, dancing away from his hand that was swinging toward her butt.

Jim narrowed his eyes, both to warn his friend off and because something was seriously fucked up. Before he could demand answers, Lillie sank to the floor in front of him, her elbows resting on his thighs as she held up Lady Luck and flashed a dazzling smile.

"Here." She tilted her head toward Damon. "I won the bet. I told him you'd turn down his gift. So now? Lady Luck is mine forever, which means she's yours too."

There should have been a playbook offered with this conversation. "I... You won Lady Luck? But Damon brought her here..."

Damon laughed. "She's way better at bartering than you, dude. Called me up the other day and suggested we do an all-or-nothing for ownership of Lady Luck. Pointed out you and I didn't need a reason to get together to do crazy things—we can do that without involving the coin. So here was the deal—I offer you the coin. If you turned me down, she won. If you accepted, you got to keep Lady for the year and then she'd legally become mine forever."

She'd gambled on him valuing her more than the trinket. Jim stroked her cheek softly. "I love you."

"I know. And you don't need any lucky coin to be happy." She rubbed her cheek against his hand, and this time when he pulled her closer she didn't refuse, rising to meet him and accept his kiss.

"And...that's my cue to take my bags to my room. You got Netflix in this place? I feel the need for a marathon of zombie movies. Or an apocalyptic Day After Tomorrow ice age washes over the earth and leaves the place looking like— well, surprise, surprise. Look outside," he exclaimed. "Just like that."

Jim brought Lillie to her feet at his side, laughingly bumping his friend. "Movie marathon if you want, or we take out the snowmobiles. Freak out the local mountain lions—have some fun."

Damon offered a hand. "You're a good man, bro. You deserve to be happy."

Like old times, Jim clasped his friend's hand firmly. "This isn't goodbye forever. You'll be out for our wedding in the spring."

"And you need to meet Addie—she'll be coming out then as well." Lillie could pull off beseeching like whoa.

"I'm defenseless against your united assault." Damon

pressed a hand to his chest. "Of course I'll be here to support you. But now? I'm gonna wipe you both off the mountainside."

Jim let his friend get ahead of them, holding Lillie back until they had privacy. She waited for him to speak, her happy glow turning her into a shimmering human statue.

"You trusted me an awful lot with that bet." Jim caught her hair in his hand, tugging her face toward him.

"Maybe, maybe not." Lillie wrapped her fingers around his neck. "I already trusted you with my heart. There's not anything bigger than that."

And that was true, and she was right.

And this was just the beginning of forever as far as he was concerned. "So, there's only one thing left to say."

She raised a brow expectantly.

"What do I win when I beat you on the trail today? I think a dirty massage works."

Lillie laughed. "With my tongue?"

Oh *fuck*. Jim adjusted his stance, his cock instantly reacting in a Pavlovian response. "*Shit.*"

She danced out of reach. "Deal. I'll even be naked the entire time. Hmmm, I might use the music I did the pole dance to in the club. Remember? I'll play it in the background."

Then she turned, her hips swaying vigorously as she hummed the dirty tune, passing Damon in the front room as Jim walked awkwardly, hindered by his body but hopelessly and utterly in love with his lady.

His luck had come home forever.

~

If you'd like to touch base with Jim and Lillie a few more months down the road, and get a hint of what's coming with Damon (and Addie!) I've added a FREE BONUS SCENE. Turn the page to enjoy the scene titled LOVERS AND FRIENDS!

LOVERS AND FRIENDS

Row after row of cardboard boxes filled the front entrance of their home, the brown cubes a stark contrast to the elegant marble and tasteful artwork gracing the walls.

Even as he paced across the wide foyer, Jim Halcyon wondered how on earth they possibly needed more of anything at this point in the wedding prep, but when Lillie stepped through the front doors to bestow a dazzling smile on him, he forgot about the mess. Forgot about the rush of people who'd soon be invading his peaceful home, forgot *everything*—except her.

His woman. His mate, happiness shining off her like the sunlight shone off her coppery-coloured hair.

She all but danced up to him, pressing the palms of her hands to his chest followed immediately by the rest of her softness as she nestled in tight and destroyed his concentration. "I think these are the last of them."

A chuckle escaped. "Are you sure? It looks like we have enough for three weddings."

She fluttered her lashes, her expression all sweet and innocent. "Maybe if I think hard enough, I can come up with something we need to order last minute, special delivery."

Jim pressed his fingers under her chin. "You could, but since we have an organizer who's managing everything and all *you're* supposed to do is enjoy yourself, I think I need to find some other way to keep you busy."

"Out of mischief, you mean," Lillie said, eyes sparkling.

Keeping her out of mischief was the last thing he wanted. She'd dropped into his life at the perfect time, in the perfect way, and from *one final fling in Vegas* to them officially tying the knot this weekend, they'd come a long way.

He held out a hand, enticing her toward the indoor swimming pool. "You've been working too hard."

"But I'm enjoying every minute of it," she insisted. "Everything we've got planned for the weekend is perfect, and I wouldn't change a thing."

He knew her well enough to hear the *except for* she'd refused to voice. It was her heart he listened to—her heart that beat in his damn chest.

Sweet, humid air hit them as they slipped through the doors. It was like a tropical paradise had been picked up and dropped into the middle of the Yukon, and in a way, it had. Comfy loungers surrounded the beautiful teardrop-shaped pool, with full sun exposure shining down on lush tropical plants in full bloom. Heaters were strategically tucked into ceiling corners for when they were needed to erase the wintry chill of the far north.

Right now, though, the early June temperatures kept their home just outside Whitehorse plenty warm enough without any help. He liked the location, and he liked the nearby city, but most of all, he'd discovered he thoroughly enjoyed being settled down. Not even the political turmoil approaching like a speeding freight train could tear the smile from his face.

Lillie seemed happy with their life together as well, and watching her get excited over their upcoming big day had made all the fuss worthwhile.

Jim sat on one of the oversized lounge chairs. She instantly crawled into his lap, settling on top of him and resting her head on his chest as if drawing encouragement and strength from listening to his heartbeat.

It beat for her. *All for her.*

Just one disappointment marred the frantic and fun plans. "You're sad your best friend can't join us for the wedding."

Her delicate fingers wrapped around his torso and she gave him a light squeeze. "You know me better than I know myself at times."

He stroked her hair, the long tresses tickling his biceps. "I've caught you. Smiling and dancing through whatever you're working on then suddenly you get distracted. Like you realize Addie's not there."

"It doesn't make sense. I mean, it's not like we lived in each other's pockets before I moved away."

"No, but you were close. And you haven't seen her in months—makes sense to me."

She pressed a quick kiss to his chest before sighing heavily. "You're right. I wish she could be here, but we're the ones who changed the date for our wedding. It wasn't fair to expect her to give up the job she'd already accepted."

Addie had rightly refused to go back on her word, in spite of sharing she'd been tempted to bail on the project. If it had just been about the money, he would've gladly thrown some at the problem to get her to come put a smile on his Lillie's face, but all three of them knew that wasn't the right thing to do. Addie needed to keep her commitment.

Didn't mean he couldn't find another solution that would make his woman happy. "She means a lot to you."

Lillie nodded, her chin brushing him. "She's always been there for me. Always had my back, even if it was just via email."

Jim was glad she was lying down, not only because the warmth of her body on top of his was oh-so-satisfying, but because this way she couldn't see him grin with anticipation.

He wanted to keep the surprise secret for a few more moments.

She traced a finger on his chest, rubbing in circles, and his entire body, his entire *self* reacted, instantly struck with a strong desire to take care of her, and an even stronger desire to be everything she needed him to be. Protector, friend...

Lover.

She tilted her head back, mischief in her eyes before she lowered her lashes and gave him a sultry come-hither look. "Did you know there's no one in the house right now?"

Jim feigned surprise. "How on earth did that happen?"

Lillie wiggled enticingly. Then she wiggled again to end up straddling him, gazing down with pure adoration. "I sent them all away."

"Whatever will we do with ourselves?"

Her tongue slipped over her lips. A deliberate taunt as she left the surface glistening with moisture. She arched her back, stretching her arms overhead. "I think I'll take a nap."

He had her under him in less than a second. Cradling himself over her as he gazed down her body hungrily. "You go right ahead. I'm going to have a snack."

Jim took her lips in a hungry, possessive kiss. She was everything he'd ever wanted. It didn't matter if he'd found her, or she'd always been his, or if she'd been sent to him—they had always been meant to be together.

~

Lillie straightened her clothing as she ducked under Jim's arm. "One vigorous *nap* is all we have time for," she teased.

He growled, but the sound was amusement and passion all tied up with infinite patience. "I can't get enough of you," he complained.

She batted her eyelashes, putting extra love into the kiss she pressed to his cheek before heading toward the front door. A rapid summons was beating like a tattoo against the heavy wood, the noise getting louder and more frantic the longer it took for her to reach the door.

This was what she got for dismissing the staff for the afternoon. She had tender spots on her body from the romp in the sunroom, and there was no chance to disguise what had to be love bites left on her neck as she hurried across the final distance and undid the lock.

The door swung open, and she put on a polite face, expecting more deliveries for the wedding,

Instead, she met the smooth brown gaze and cheery smile of her best friend. That's all she had time to see in the second before Addie threw herself forward and entangled Lillie in an enormous hug.

The rib-cracking embrace plus the thrill of excitement made it hard to breathe, let alone shout in delight.

"Holy moly. Holy *moly*." Lillie squeezed her friend, released her, then squeezed once more just because she couldn't believe Addie was real. She pushed her away as shocked amazement rushed her system. "I thought you couldn't come to the wedding."

Addie caught hold of Lillie's forearms, swinging their arms back and forth as if they were children. "I can't. I've only got two days before my next job starts, but Jim said you needed me, so I'm here."

Lillie's heart already belonged to the big bear, but after this, he'd bought himself forgiveness for a multitude of sins during the years to come. "Jim flew you out for *two days?*"

"Yup."

"All the way from Scotland?"

"Yup."

Lillie shook her head even as she tugged Addie with her farther into the house. "You're going to be jet-lagged the entire time," she scolded. "You could've come to visit some other time. You didn't have to come now."

Addie shrugged, gazing around the house. "So I'll drink a little extra coffee, I don't mind. I wanted to see you, and I wanted to see your house, and if I have to stay awake for forty-eight hours, it won't be the first time."

Lillie laughed. "No, it won't. Remember when..."

The day passed in a whirl. Lillie showed off her beautiful home and estate above Whitehorse while stories and good memories passed back and forth between them. The time was perfect and wonderful and everything she could've hoped for.

She stood beside their bed that night, looking down at the man who was about to become her husband. The man who was already hers in all the best ways. "Thank you."

They were mere words, but they were enough because he knew what she was truly saying.

He patted the bed and Lillie slipped beside him. "I like

your Addie. She's fierce, and funny, and exactly how I imagined your best friend would be."

Lillie sat up on her knees as she linked her fingers with his. "She's my perfect best friend, and I'm so glad she's here. Although I am sorry she's not staying long enough for Damon to meet her."

Her not-so-casual mention of Jim's perfect best friend brought a smile to his lips. "I don't know. Putting those two together sounds an awful lot like matchmaking to me."

Lillie fluttered her lashes. "Whatever are you insinuating?"

He lifted her hand to his mouth and kissed her knuckles. "You know it's true. Admit it. If you could, you would make *everyone* find someone. I've seen the way you look at Damon."

What? She didn't look at anyone except the big bear beside her with interest, and she was sure he knew that. She plopped her fists on her hips and stared at him in confusion. "How do I look at him?" she demanded.

"As if he's a trophy to be handed out."

"Oops." Guilty as charged. "It's only because I want everyone to be as happy as we are." She kept her expression as innocent as possible.

Somehow. Mostly.

His lips twitched. "Really?"

They both rumbled off into laughter, not because what they had wasn't the most perfect thing, but because they didn't need platitudes. They didn't need *anything* but each other.

"Yeah, you caught me." Lillie confessed. "I'm sad I can't match-make, but if them being together is the right thing, fate will make it happen without my help." She leaned forward and pressed her lips to his. "Thank you for my present. I love you."

He wrapped his hand around the back of her head, drawing her to him as he answered with another kiss.

~

Email from: Addie MacShay
Delivery to: Lillie Halcyon

Lousy Internet. If you don't get this, let me know. ;)

Seriously, I'm sending this message through a dozen different channels in the hopes one of them makes it—communication is so bad I considered slipping a note in a bottle to see if that reaches you first.

Cell phone coverage sucks big time, and there's no Internet at all at the manor—you'd die up here in this remote part of the Scottish highlands, Hacker Girl. Good thing you got that big, brawny, very rich mate of yours who installed unlimited satellite access up there in your Yukon boonies for you.

We won't talk about the other things he's giving you on a regular basis. I'm not even going to think about the last time I got to get up close and personal with someone big and brawny who looks at me like I hung the moon.

Glad to hear everything went well with your wedding. You looked gorgeous in the pictures you sent, and Jim was handsome enough to take my breath away. And that blond friend of his, the wolf? Arwhooooooo! Don't I wish I could have stayed to get some of that!

Enough of me drooling.

Short update: Job is okay, people at the jobsite are weird. Sums up my life.

Longer story: the actual job is going great. Interestingly, I found an additional will the day after I started. Not so cool—now both of the possible heirs have decided to move back into the castle. I have cat-shifters staring at me throughout the day, oh joy, oh bliss.

Dealing with them is not fun, but the estate itself is beautiful. I'll figure out some way to keep them from creeping me out, so don't you worry. You enjoy your honeymoon with that growly bear of yours. Remind him if he doesn't treat you right, I'm coming over and finding out all his dirty secrets to use as blackmail material.

Who am I kidding? The guy is head over heels for you. I'd be jealous if I didn't love you so much, BFF.

Stay safe. Let me know if you get this, otherwise, I'll be in touch if I need anything.

<3

Addie

~

Email from: Addie MacShay
Delivery to: Lillie Halcyon

They are creeeeeeeeeeeping me ouuuuuuuuuuuuut. Like, omg. I've moved rooms

~

Email from: Addie MacShay
Delivery to: Lillie Halcyon

If you got that email, ignore it. I didn't mean to send it. I mean, I wrote it, and they're creepy, but I hit send accidentally, and nothing is bad, but... I don't want you to worry, so never mind. I'll be fine.

I sure miss you, though, bestie. I'll be very glad when this job is over.

Stupid Internet.

<3 you, teddybear girl
Addie

~

Lillie stared at the most recent messages from her friend for a long, long time, the sensation of dread in her gut refusing to fade. Of course, Addie didn't want her to worry. Of course, her bestie would be fine.

But...

Maybe...

Warm lips pressed to the back of her neck. "You said you were coming to bed an hour ago. What's got you all distracted?"

She twirled the chair so she could reach up and drape her arms around Jim's neck, stroking her fingers into his thick hair. "Worried about Addie," she admitted.

He nodded solemnly. She'd told him about the emails. He knew something wasn't right. "Just say the word. I care about her, too."

"You don't think I'm being overdramatic?"

Jim tucked his hands under her and lifted her from the chair. "Nope. So, let's call in the dogs of war. Dog of war. Whatever."

She laughed, her fears fading as she wrapped herself

around him, palms cupping his face. Happiness rolled back in, and she had to tease. "I'm telling Damon you called him names."

"Dog? He knows. I owe him for that Teddy Ruxpin he slipped into your luggage. *I'm* the only bear you get to cuddle from now on."

"I love you," she whispered.

"Of course you do. I'm the most loveable bear in the room. Actually, after I threw Teddy out the window, I'm the *only* bear in the room." He chuckled as she rolled her eyes, carefully depositing her on the bed before grabbing his phone off the bedside dresser

Lillie eavesdropped as he made contact with his best friend, reassured that Addie would get some help, soon. That's what mattered the most right now. Friends...

...and her lover, her *husband*, who was hanging up after a remarkably short conversation.

"That's it? You say he needs to go to Scotland, and he goes?"

Jim replaced the phone on the dresser without looking, the case clattering on the surface while his gaze remained locked on her body. "I said 'Lillie wants you to go'. Like he was going to argue. Changing the subject, when did you get naked?"

Being a shifter meant being good at ditching clothing.

"Am I naked?" she murmured as if surprised. "Oh, dear. I suppose I should do something about that."

"I have a few ideas..."

He pounced. All six foot plus of massive grizzly bear-shifter, which made the mattress recoil like the surface of a trampoline. Lillie bounced skyward before landing in his arms, which was fine by her.

It was exactly where she belonged.

~

New York Times Bestselling Author Vivian Arend
brings you a series of light-hearted,
stand-alone novellas filled with shifters of all kinds—bears,
wolves, lynx. Whether they're fated mates or falling head-
over-paws, there's always a happily-ever-after.

~

Takhini Shifters
Copper King
Laird Wolf
A Lady's Heart
Wild Prince

~

ABOUT THE AUTHOR

New York Times and *USA Today* bestselling author Vivian Arend loves to share the products of her over-active imagination with her readers. She writes contemporary, western, and light-hearted paranormal romances. The stories are humorous yet emotional, usually with a large cast of family or friends, and a guaranteed happily-ever-after.

Vivian lives in British Columbia, Canada, with her husband of many years—her inspiration for every hero and a willing companion for all sorts of adventures.

Find out more at www.vivianarend.com.

www.ingramcontent.com/pod-product-compliance
Lightning Source LLC
Chambersburg PA
CBHW031001210726
48290CB00007B/2412